Atlas Publishing Co., S. Wangersheim

Illustrated Atlas and Columbian Souvenir of Branch County,

Michigan

including a directory of free holders of the county - Vol. 1

Atlas Publishing Co., S. Wangersheim

Illustrated Atlas and Columbian Souvenir of Branch County, Michigan
including a directory of free holders of the county - Vol. 1

ISBN/EAN: 9783337286507

Printed in Europe, USA, Canada, Australia, Japan

Cover: Foto ©Andreas Hilbeck / pixelio.de

More available books at **www.hansebooks.com**

ILLUSTRATED

ATLAS

AND

Columbian Souvenir

OF

BRANCH COUNTY,

MICHIGAN,

Including a directory of free holders of the County, compiled, and published from
official records and personal examination by

———◦◦◦◦———

THE ATLAS PUBLISHING COMPANY,
FORT WAYNE, INDIANA
1894.

TABLE OF CONTENTS.

ILLUSTRATIONS.

OUTLINE
MAP OF
BRANCH COUNTY
MICHIGAN.

MAP OF
SHERWOOD

Township 5 South   Range 8 West

MAP OF
UNION

Township 5 South   Range 7 West

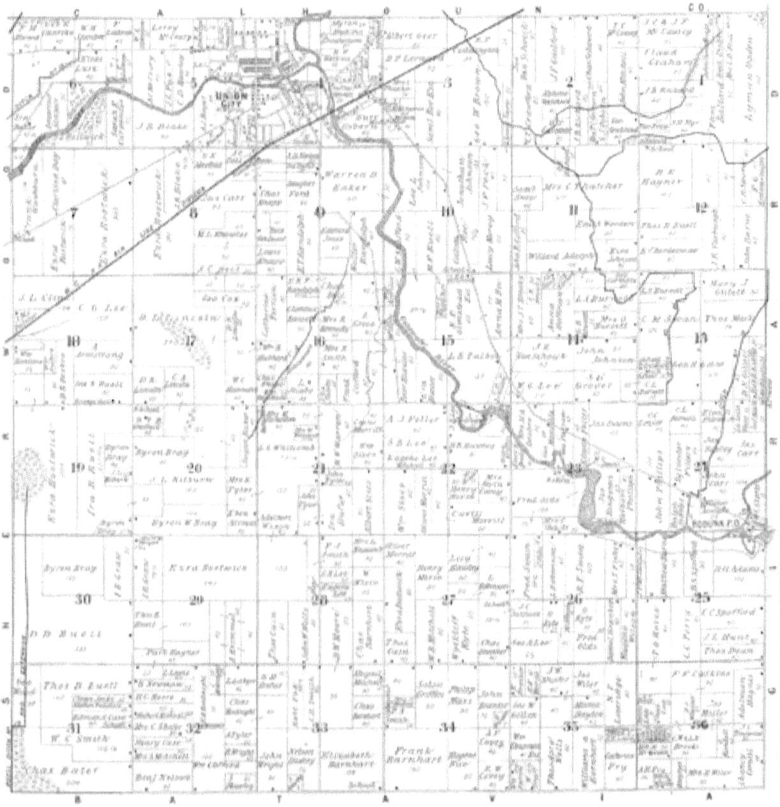

MAP OF

GIRARD

Township 5 South   Range 6 West

MAP OF
BUTLER

Township 5 South   Range 5 West

MAP OF
MATTESON

Township 6 South.   Range 8 West.

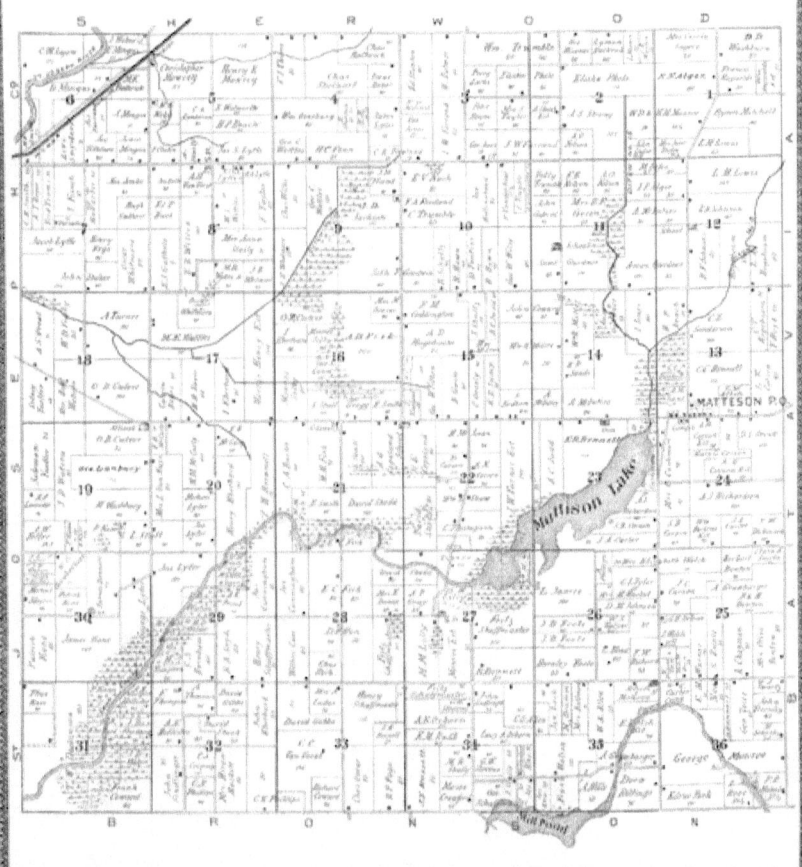

MAP OF
BATAVIA

Township 6 South   Range 7 West

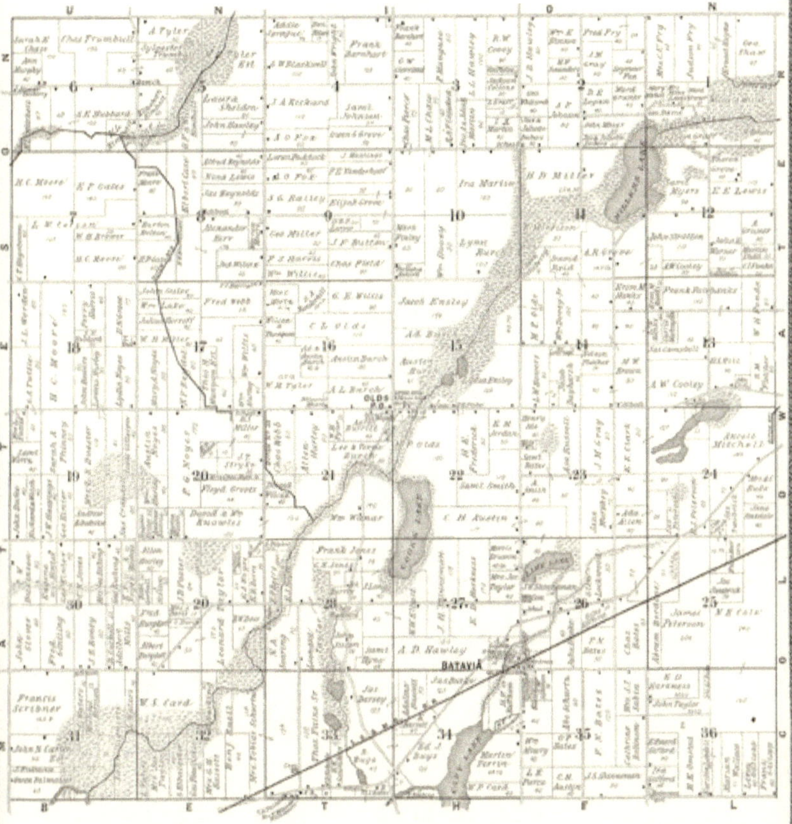

MAP OF
COLDWATER

Township 6 South   Range 6 West

MAP OF
QUINCY

Township 6 South   Range 5 West

MAP OF
BRONSON

Township 7 South   Range 8 West

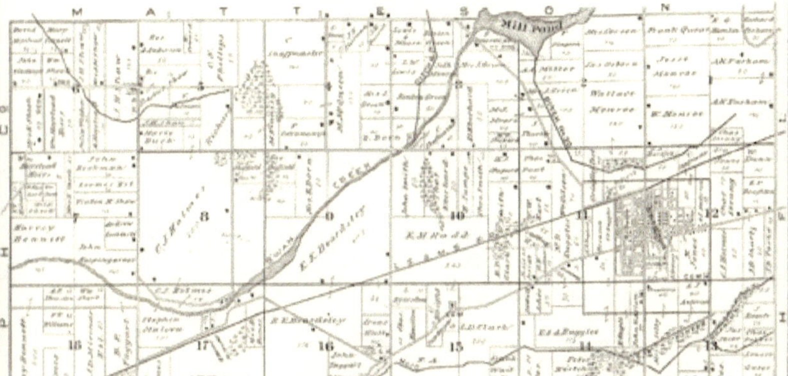

MAP OF
BETHEL
Township 7 South   Range 7 West

MAP OF OVID

Township 7 South Range 6 West

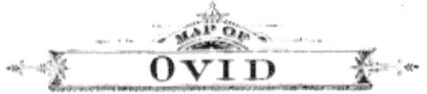

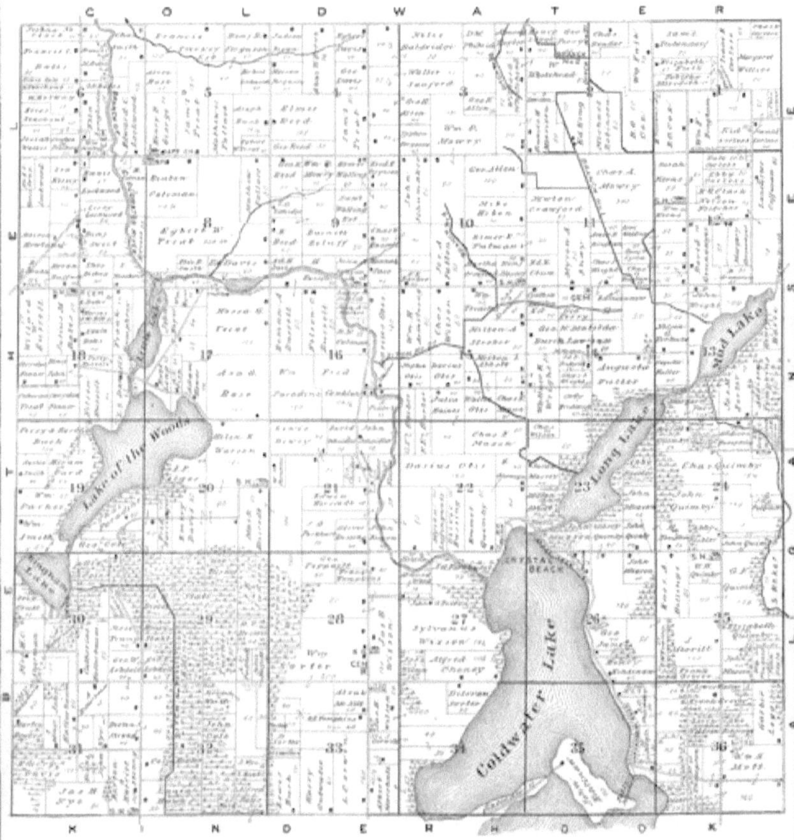

ALGANSEE

Township 7 South   Range 5 West

MARBE LAKE

MIDDLE LAKE

NOBLE

Township 8 South   Range 8 West

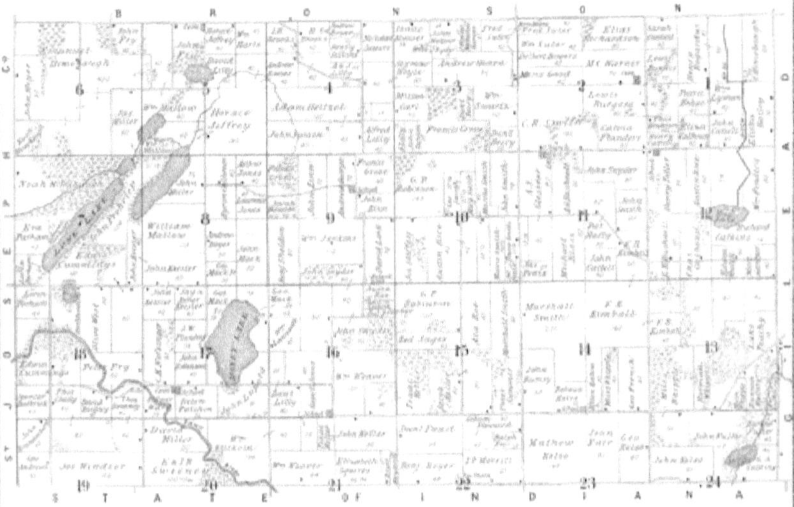

HERRICKVILLE

MAP OF
GILEAD

Township 8 South   Range 7 West

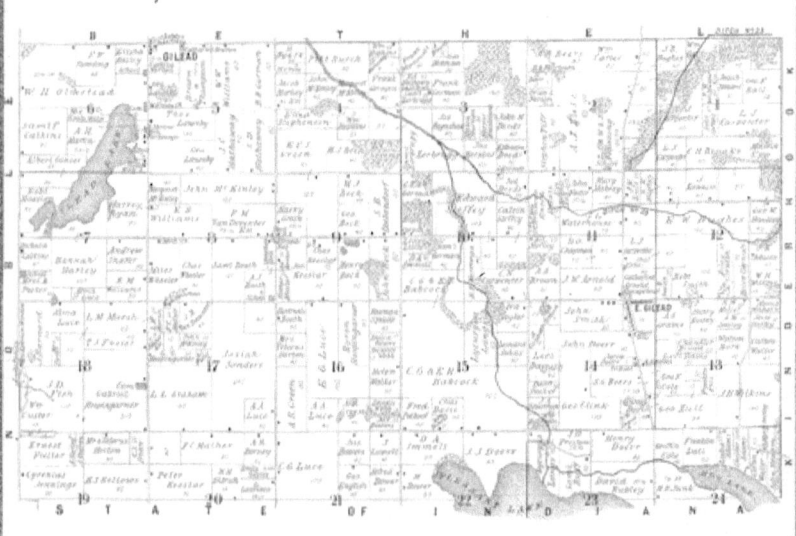

MAP OF

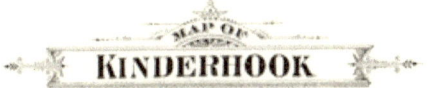

KINDERHOOK

Township 8 South   Range 6 West

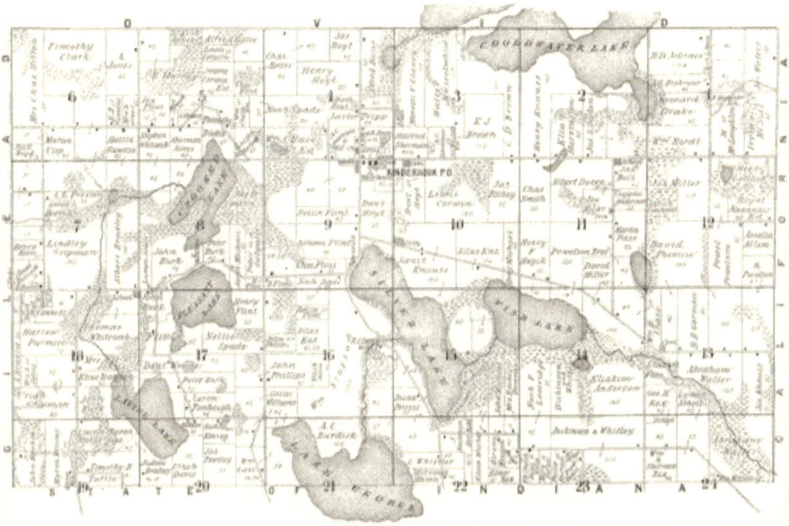

MAP OF
CALIFORNIA

Township 8 South   Range 5 West

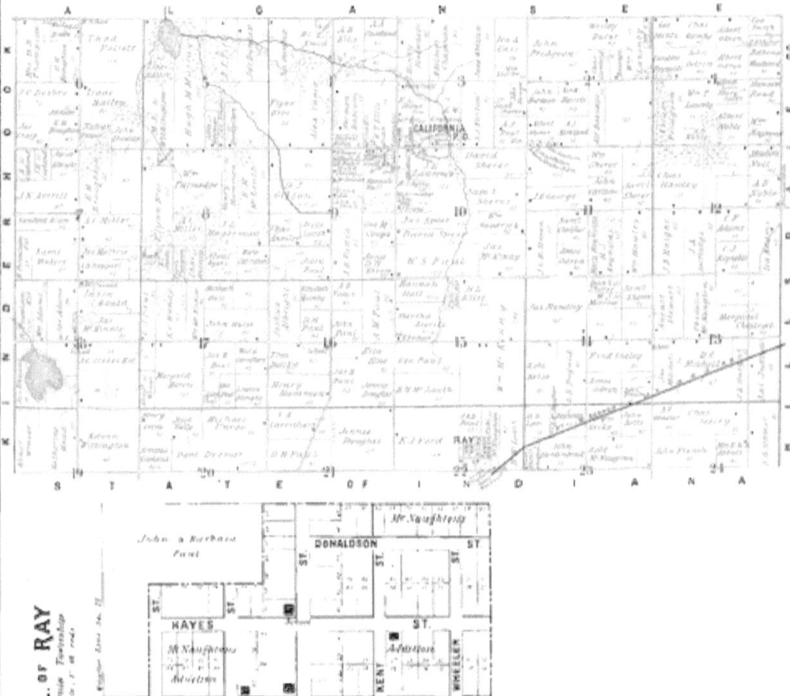

VILL. OF RAY

Outline Plan
OF
COLDWATER

Scale 60 Rods to an inch

FAIR
GROUNDS

3

2

Sec 17

Sec 16

Sec 15

4

1

Sec 20

Sec 22

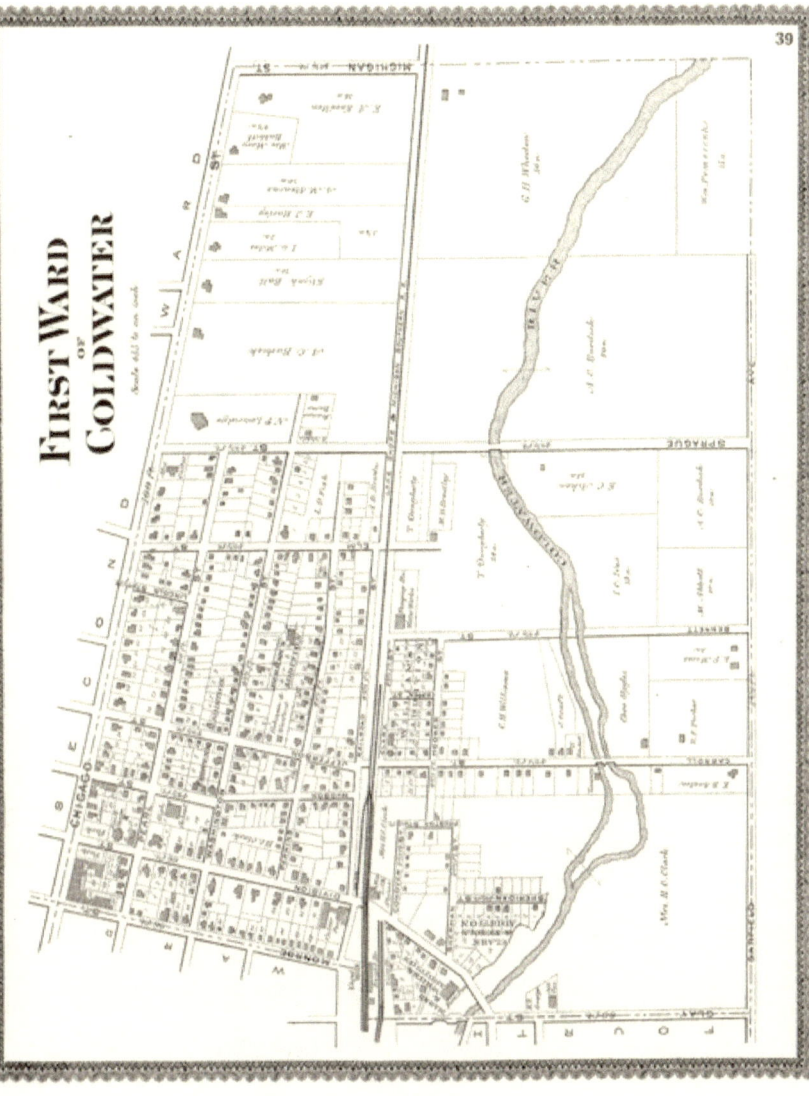

FIRST WARD
OF
GOLDWATER

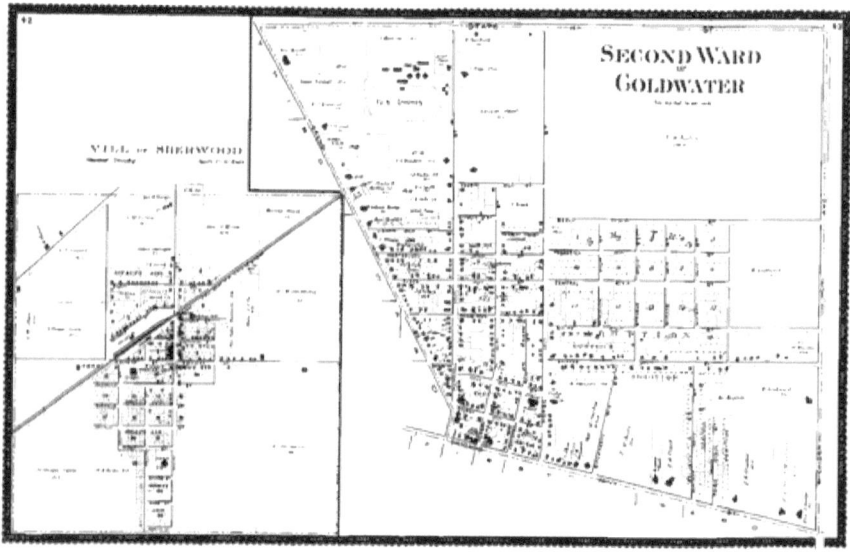

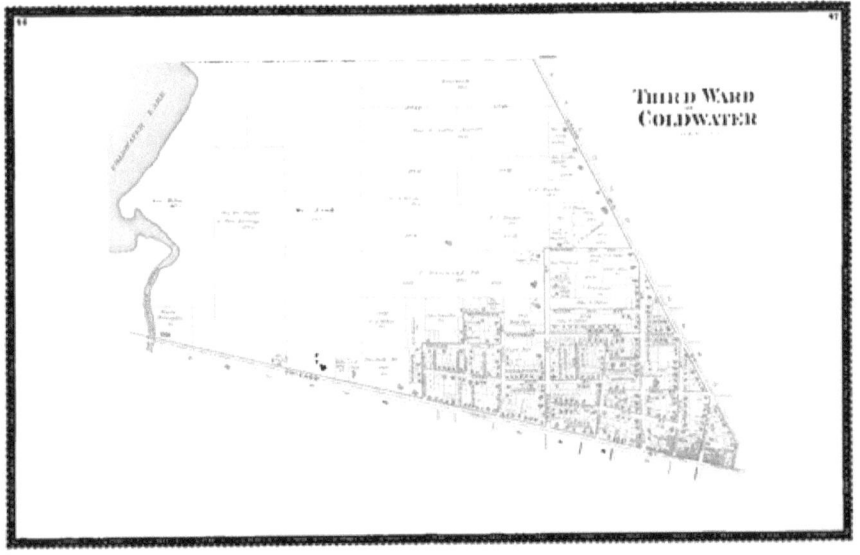

THIRD WARD
COLDWATER

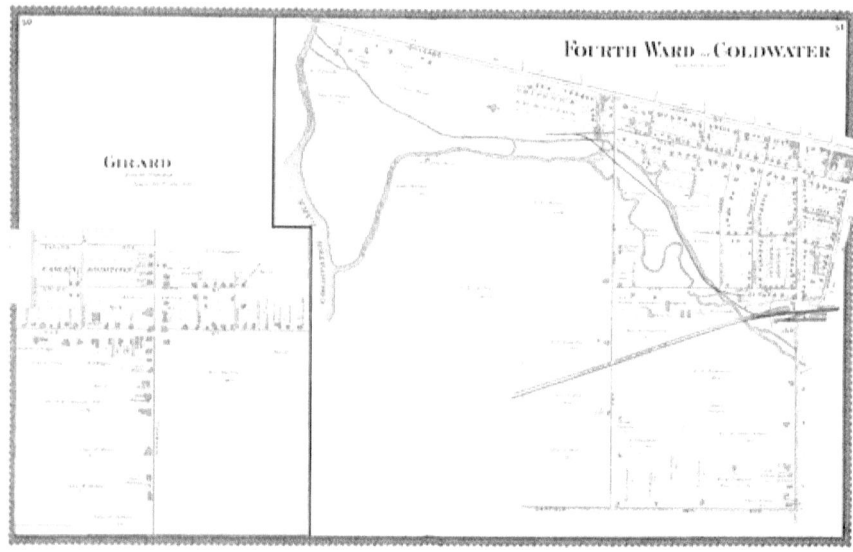

GIRARD

FOURTH WARD of COLDWATER

UNION CITY

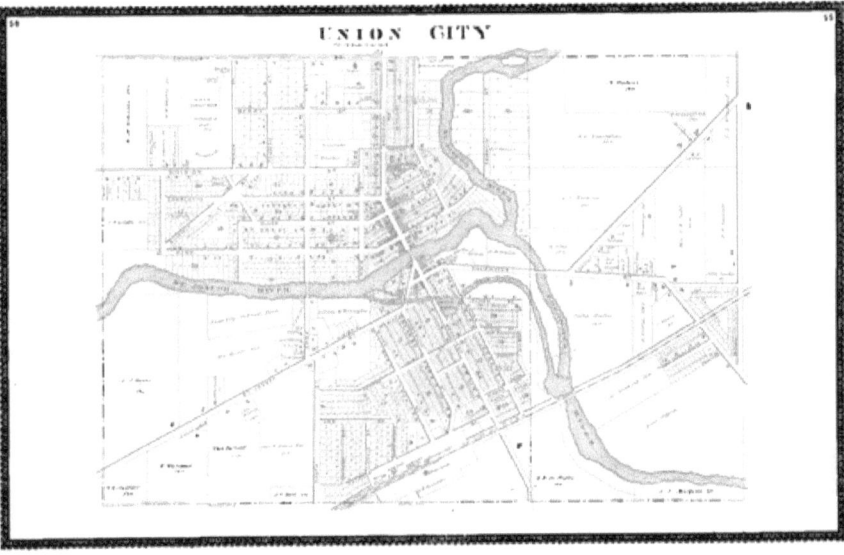

QUINCY

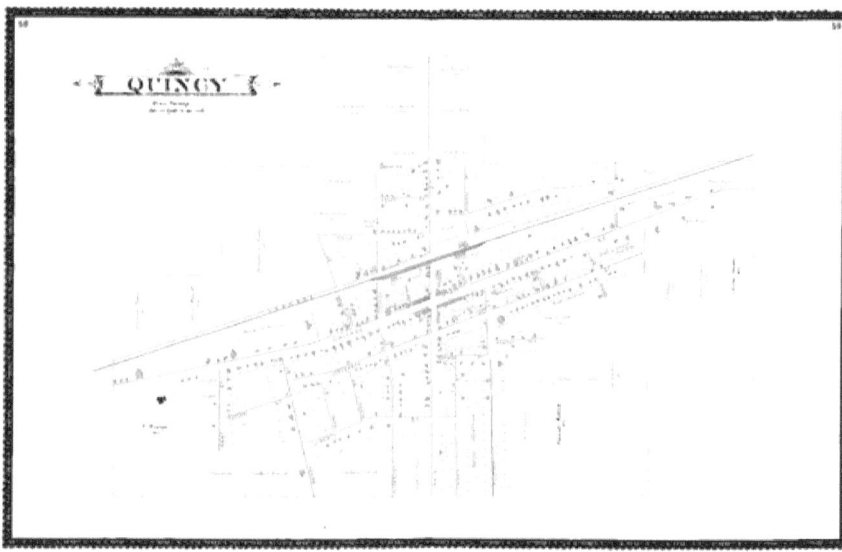

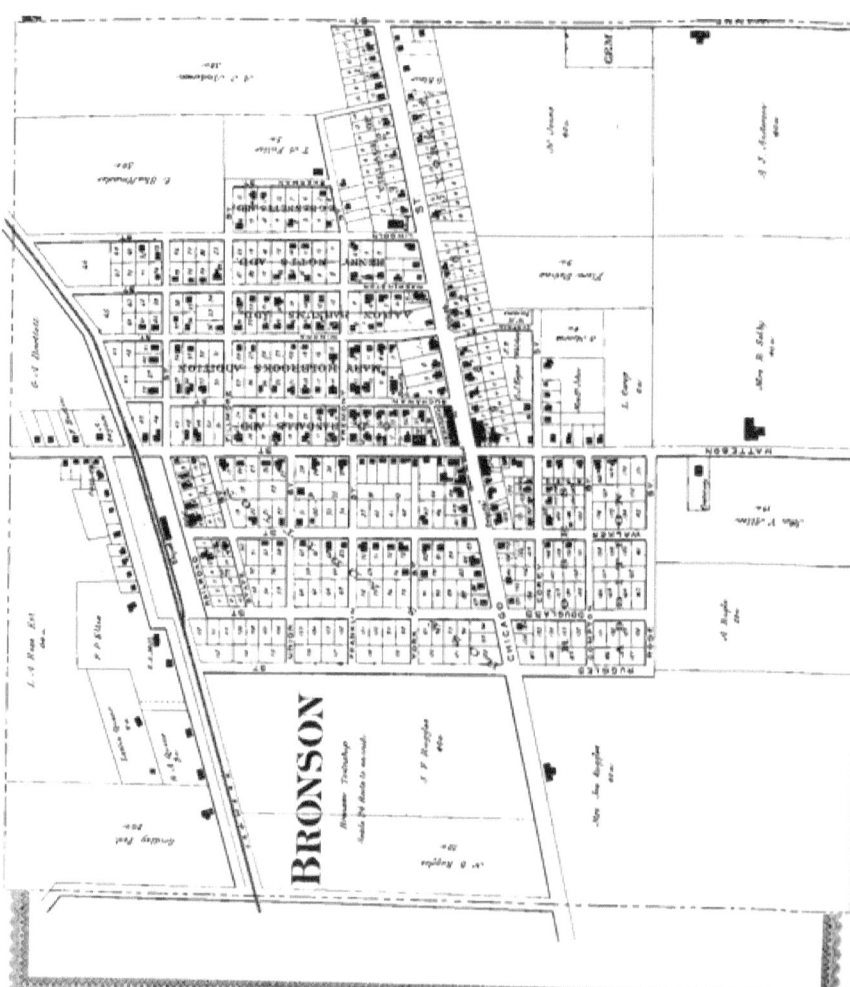

BRONSON

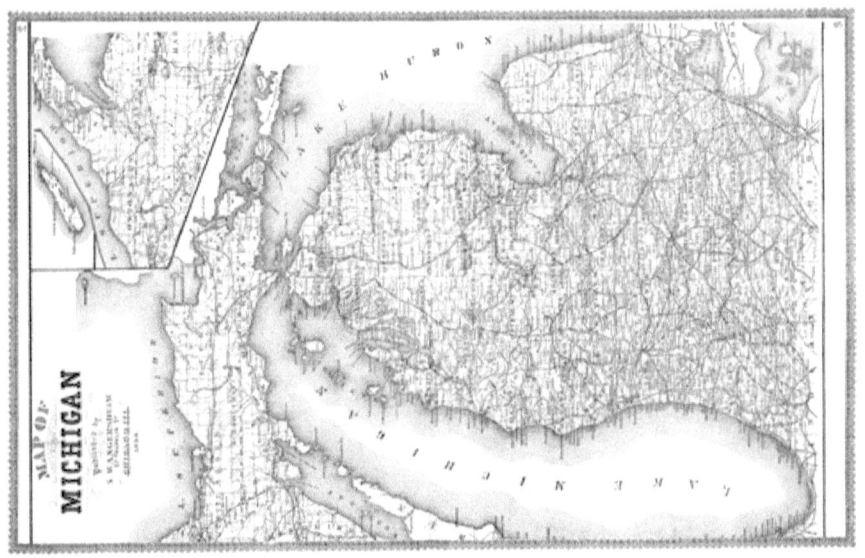

MAP OF
MICHIGAN

Street Scenes and Public Buildings, of Coldwater, Michigan.

BRANCH COUNTY, MICHIGAN.

Missing
page

Missing page

Brief Sketches

OF SOME OF

Branch County's Representative Citizens.

"A" Mill   Residence   Elevator
"B" Mill   View of Office   "C" Mill
       W. A. Coombs

PROPERTY OF W. A. COOMBS, COLDWATER, MICH.

Craig, Samuel, deceased, the subject of this sketch, was one of the pioneers of Branch Co., Michigan. He was born in the county of Armagh, Ireland, on Feb. 21, 1793. He was of Scotch ancestry, a Presbyterian in faith and a farmer by occupation. In 1818 emigrated to America, and in 1823 was united in marriage to Elizabeth Downs. A few years after his marriage, with his wife and three children, Mr. Craig started for the wilds of Michigan, stopping first at Detroit. There procuring an ox team, they began their overland journey for what was then known as the territory of Michigan. This journey was attended by many trials and privations, and a detailed sketch of it would prove of interest to many of the pioneers of the county, and we regret that a limited space will not allow us to embrace the same. Suffice to say that in 1831 Mr. Craig became the owner of eighty acres of land in Girard township, Branch Co., Mich., the title of this land being signed by Andrew Jackson then president of the United States and which is now held by the surviving members of his family, Mary Jane and Eliza Craig. Mr. Craig's death occurred March 1, 1834, and his wife on Dec. 21, 1876. They were the parents of six children, Mary Jane, James, David, Daniel, Samuel and Eliza. The old homestead is now owned and operated by his daughters, Mary Jane and Eliza. These ladies are successful farmers and prove that women are as capable as the other sex when given similar opportunities. They are engaged in general farming and make a specialty of dairying, producing yearly a large quantity of Gilt Edge butter.

Culp, John W., farmer. Came from Lockport, N. Y., and settled in Girard township in the year 1839, and bought the farm where he now resides in 1861. He was formerly in dry goods business in the city of Coldwater, after which he traveled as salesman for a wholesale house. Moved on his farm in the year 1873. Is at present Justice of the Peace; has been a Mason since 1853, also has been an Odd Fellow. He makes a specialty of breeding fine wool sheep. His farm is under excellent cultivation, has good farm buildings and produces more than the average yield from his crops; also grows all kinds of fruits produced in this climate.

Culver, O. B., farmer and small fruit raiser of Mattison township, now living on the farm where he was raised. He has about ten acres of small fruit and extensively produces plants, strawberries, blackberries, raspberries, gooseberries, and various other kinds. Has filled offices of Township Clerk and Supervisor a number of years. Is owner of three hundred and twenty acres of fine farming land, two hundred acres of which is under cultivation.

Curtis, Horace, was born in Cortland county, N. Y., August 2d, 1831, lived there until 1852 when he came to Butler township and settled on his present farm of one hundred and twenty acres on Section 15, where by industry he has carved out a fine home. His father, now deceased, was born in Essex county, N. Y. His mother was Barbara A. Curtis. Our subject married Miss Wealthy Jane Woods, who was born in Cortland county, N. Y., September 30th, 1832. From this union six children have been born. Of the one hundred and twenty acres owned by Mr. Curtis, ninety-six are under cultivation, producing full average crops. He is a member of the Board of Review and of the Farmers' Alliance, also of the F. & A. M.

David, C. Ambrose, was born December 5th, 1842, in Geauga county, Ohio, where he remained until eight years of age, when his parents came to Butler township, Branch county. Mr. David was married to Miss Jennie Faxon, of Girard township, March 15th, 1866. They are the parents of one son and two daughters, all of whom are living at home with their parents. The subject of our sketch served as soldier in the Union army during the war of the rebellion, in 1st Regiment Battery G, Light Artillery, serving three years, and during that time was engaged in the battles of Richmond, Ky., Buzzards' Roost, Atlanta, Ga., and other battles. Also was at the siege of Nashville, Tenn. Is a man highly respected by his neighbors. He makes a business of general farming. He belongs to the G. A. R., and is a member of the Grange of his township. The wife of our subject is postmistress of Faxon P. O.

Davis, J. S., Bronson, is a blacksmith by trade. After learning his trade he returned to Bronson, working at it until August, 1873, when he established his present business on Matteson street, north of the Clark House. He is owner of two good houses and lots in Bronson, is a Past Master Workman, also has filled offices of the village at different times.

Dean, Edward, resident of Girard, blacksmith by occupation. Is now carrying on the trade in the same shop where his father first started in the same business in the year 1843. Mr. Dean is an enterprising citizen and has a lucrative business.

Denham, Cornelius was born in Conway, Mass., Dec. 16, 1816, moving with his parents to Ontario county, N. Y., in the year 1818, where his father died in the year 1828. The subject of this sketch came to Butler township in the year 1865 and has resided there since. He now owns three hundred and twenty-five acres of land, two hundred and forty-five acres of which are under cultivation. He has good buildings, makes a specialty of raising fine blooded sheep and does a general farming business. He married Miss Sarah Blodgett of Ontario county, N. Y., and to this union have been born three children, one son and two daughters, all living in Branch county.

Dewsnbery, Oscar, resident of Bronson, owns a nice farm of sixty acres two miles south of Bronson. In addition to his vocation as farmer he is also dealer in agricultural implements, being agent for Arbuckle, Ryan & Co., manufacturers of farm machinery. He also follows business of threshing crops for farmers in his vicinity, owning considerable machinery for this business. He is an energetic and industrious man, respected by his neighbors.

Dobson, O. L., Quincy, Mich., engaged in the agricultural implement business about two years ago and has already built up an extensive trade. Mr. Dobson carries the Walter A. Wood binders and mowers, Dowagiac Shoe drills, Superior drills, harrows, wagons, buggies and plows. Also makes a specialty of repairs of all kinds, deals in binder twine, lubricating and illuminating oils. Has two large warehouses and is also a heavy dealer in hay, pressing and shipping large quantities to the eastern markets. Is married and has one child.

Dorrance, Albert A., present postmaster of Coldwater, Mich., is a native of the state of New York, his birthplace being in Orleans county. He finished his education in the Collegiate Institute, Brockport, N. Y. He soon after came to Detroit. In the spring of 1858 removed to Jackson, Michigan, and in 1859, being a printer, started the "Jackson Citizen," a weekly paper. At this time he was also deputy United States marshal. During the winter of 1858 and 1859 he was also a foreman of the State printing office at Lansing. Disposing of his paper to Col. Deland, after an absence of a year or more in Washington, D. C., and New York, he again returned to live in Jackson until 1869, when he came to Coldwater and purchased a drug business, in which he has continued up to the present time, now under the firm name of A. A. Dorrance & Son. In 1889 he was appointed postmaster by President Harrison, and has faithfully served the people in that capacity. It was through his efforts that the office was given a free delivery system, and has also added three daily Star routes from the office. This postoffice distributes for sixteen Star route offices. For ten years during his residence in Jackson he held the office of assistant keeper of the State Prison. For about ten years since residing in Coldwater, he has served as a member of the board of education, and a part of that time president of the same. He has been quite successful in business, and commands the respect of all who know him.

Draper, O. W. The subject of this mention, Mr. O. W. Draper, is a native of Huron county, Ohio. In 1833 came to Michigan with his parents and located on the farm which he now owns. His father, Reuben Draper still resides here having reached the ripe old age of ninety-three years. Our subject, Mr. O. W. Draper was educated in the schools of this county and has been a lifelong resident of Algansee township. In 1862 he enlisted in the 1st Michigan Sharpshooters and served until the close of the war. In 1866 he was elected school inspector and served as such for two years. On his return from the war he was elected township clerk and filled that position for eight years. Again in 1879 he was elected supervisor from Algansee township and served until 1883, afterward appointed to fill the unexpired term of M. B. Wakeman, who was elected register of deeds. Mr. Draper is considered one of the solid men of Branch county. He is the owner of a good farm and has made a success of farming, his wheat yield running from eighteen to twenty bushels per acre, corn from fifty to seventy. He is one of the leading members of the G. A. R., also of the Congregational church.

Ewing & Portner, proprietors of the Coldwater Marble and Granite Works. The firm was organized by Mr. Charles Ewing and W. A. Portner in the year 1883. They do a general business in stone work and have erected some of the finest monuments in Southern Michigan and Northern Indiana besides doing a general business in stone work for public buildings, etc. Mr. Ewing, the senior member of the firm, has served the people as alderman for the second ward, and Mr. Portner, the junior member of the firm, has taken an active interest in the city affairs, being at the present time chief of the fire department which he assisted to organize in 1888.

Fay, G. E., Quincy, was born in 1869, three miles from Quincy, attended the schools of his place and by close attention to his studies obtained a liberal education. Mr. Fay is engaged in handling well material, wind pumps, steam fittings and general plumbing business, which he established in 1891. Has a good stock and increasing trade.

Fenn, J. W., real estate and insurance, Coldwater. Established business April 1, 1893, previous to which time he was engaged in farming and at present, in addition to his business in this city, carries on a general farming business, managing over three hundred acres of land in Coldwater township. He is doing a general real estate business in city and farm property, also a general life and fire insurance business.

Ferguson, W. C., Coldwater, is one of the successful farmers of Branch county. He came from Newport, N. Y., in 1853. Bought the farm where he now resides, which by hard work he has made one of the best farms in Branch county. Mr. Ferguson takes a deep interest in sheep growing, the Shropshires being his favorite strain. He was married to Elizabeth Noble, thirty-nine years ago. To this union have been born three sons, all living. The subject of this sketch has expended three thousand dollars on his farm for improvements.

First National Bank, Quincy, Michigan. This is one of the best known banking houses in Branch county. It was organized in September, 1881, with a capital stock of $50,000 and now has a surplus and undivided profits of $10,000, making in all $60,000. The present officers of the bank are C. H. Winchester, pres., J. H. Jones, vice-pres., C. L. Truesdell, cash. This bank has done a large and profitable business since its organization and much credit is due its efficient and genial cashier, Mr. C. L. Truesdell, whose experience in banking affairs dates back several years. He is one of the well-known men of Quincy, and the straightforward manner in which he has conducted the business has won for him many warm personal friends and the respect and confidence of the entire community.

Fisk, J. D. W., Coldwater, has resided in the county since the year 1835. He is engaged as general farmer, taking considerable interest in raising small fruits and dairying. Mr. Fisk served for fifteen years as secretary of the County Agricultural Society and at the present time is president of the same. He is one of Branch county's successful men, being well and favorably known throughout the county. Since the above sketch was written Mr. Fisk has died, his death taking place in December, 1893. By his demise Branch county has lost one of its best citizens, a man highly respected by all who knew him.

Fisk, Samuel, residing in the township of Coldwater, came to Michigan in 1867 and located upon the farm he now owns, where he has since followed the occupation of general farmer. Mr. Fisk has been successful in all respects, having a large farm which is under the highest state of cultivation and with the best of improvements. He is a man highly esteemed by his neighbors who have called upon him to represent them in official capacities, having served continuously as township treasurer since 1887 and is now also filling the office of supervisor of Coldwater township. He is a native of the state of N. Y.

Flint, Henry P., Kinderhook, was born in the year 1848 in the township of Eckford, Calhoun county, Michigan. At the age of three years his parents moved to Kinderhook, Branch county where he has resided ever since. At the age of twenty-three, and in the year 1871 he was married to Miss Mary Kee, also of Kinderhook. They have as a result of this marriage four children, three boys and one girl, at the time of this writing all living. He has a farm of one hundred and forty acres of good land which he has cleared and improved mostly himself with comfortable buildings.

Flint, Ira A., a prosperous farmer of Kinderhook township was born in Calhoun county, Michigan, in 1847, and continued to reside in that county until he was six years of age. His parents at that time moved to Branch county and settled in Kinderhook township on section nine. It was here our subject resided until he reached his majority. In 1868 he was united in marriage to Miss Ida Hovey. He then settled in Kinderhook township and has continued to reside here since that time. He has an excellent farm of one hundred and fifteen acres, beautifully situated on the bank of Flint Lake. His buildings are of modern style and well arranged for convenience. Mr. Flint has been successful as a farmer and is recognized as one of the best in Kinderhook township.

T. A. SHILTON, THE BEST CLOTHIER,
COLDWATER, MICH.

PORTRAIT AND RESIDENCE OF A. A. DORRANCE, COLDWATER, MICH.

in Battle Creek, Mich., at which point his father died in the year 1844. Two years later his mother married John Bradley and came to Kinderhook township, locating on section 7. The subject of sketch was obliged to shift for himself at an early age, working upon farms at small wages, but taking advantage of every opportunity to acquire an education. In early manhood he would do farm work during the summer months and taught school during the winters. His first school, at the age of nineteen, was what is known as the Loon Lake school in the township of Angola, Steuben county, Indiana. He took up the trade of carpenter at which he worked in summers and continued to teach school winters up to the year 1862, when he married Francis A. Purdy, of the township of Kinderhook. In the fall of 1865 they moved to the farm upon which they now reside. He has followed the occupation of general farmer since that time and has made for himself and family a beautiful home with all of the modern improvements, surrounded by an abundance of fruit and ornamental trees in place of the tall oak that occupied the ground where the buildings now stand.

Griswold, Martin A., farmer, residing in Algansee township, was born in the same township Feb. 18, 1867 where he has resided ever since. Was married to Miss Ella Hoyt, also a native of Algansee township in 1886. Is owner of 77½ acres of land, fifty of which are under cultivation, yielding an average wheat crop of eighteen bushels per acre, and of corn, forty bushels, other farm crops in proportion. Mr. and Mrs. Griswold are active members of the M. E. Church. His father, Aaron Griswold, was a native of the state of New York, where he was born in the year 1828, residing there until 1863 when he came to Hillsdale county, Michigan, afterward moving to Algansee township, where he died in 1886.

Grube, H. A. Dr., physician of Coldwater, is a native of Indiana, born in Plymouth, Marshall county. He received his education in the schools of that city and began the study of medicine in 1888 in the University of Michigan, graduating from there in the year 1891. He is a general practitioner, with special attention to the diseases of children. He began practice in Coldwater the same year that he graduated and has continued since that time. He served one year as attending physician for the State school and two years as county physician. He gives his whole time and attention to the practice of his profession.

Guthrie, F. J., Colon, is a farmer by occupation. Is a native of the state of Ohio and came to Mattison township in 1870. He has served the people as justice of the peace for four years. He is a member of the Grange Society, also of the Farmers' Alliance.

Hall, J. C. & Son, livery, feed and sale stable, No. 158 South Monroe street, Coldwater. Mr. J. C. Hall has been engaged in the livery business in this city for over twenty-five years, giving his whole time and attention to the same, doing a general livery business. Mr. Hall has served as deputy sheriff, constable and collector for a number of years.

Harrington, John, resident of Butler township, was born in Summit county, Ohio, Nov. 8, 1825, and resided there until he was twenty-two years of age when he came to Hillsdale county, Mich. He then moved again to the state of New York, but in 1873 returned to Butler township, Branch county, and purchased the farm upon which he now resides. His farm consists of eighty acres, fifty of which are under cultivation. He also has buildings of fine character. Is engaged in general farming pursuits. The subject of this sketch married Miss Sarah C. Fincher, on November 28, 1862, a native of Ogden, Monroe county, New York, born October 12, 1833. They are parents of two sons, one now living at home, the other being employed as a locomotive engineer.

Hass, George B., resident of Sherwood and engaged in farming pursuits. He is a native of St. Joseph county, coming to Sherwood in 1876, purchasing the farm upon which he now resides. His farm consists of ninety acres which is well improved, and is also owner of good farm buildings. He has filled the office of treasurer of his township, two terms, also as director in the Farmers' Insurance company of Branch county. Was a member of the late Michigan 17th Infantry Vet Vols., serving two years and five months.

Hawley, William, resident of California township, was born in Dundee, N. Y., August 29, 1843. His parents came to Michigan when he was seven years of age, settling at first in Hillsdale county, and later came into California township, which has been Mr. Hawley's residence since. Early in life he was married to Sarah Taft, now deceased, and to which union one daughter was born. He was again married September 11, 1892, to Mrs. Emma Reed, a native of Knoxville, Tenn. Mr. Hawley owns eighty acres of fine farm land and is doing a general farming business. He has held some of the offices of his township.

Herendeen, William W., resident of Quincy, is one of the enterprising business men of the village and of Branch county. He has owned and operated a livery barn for eight years and is owner of the only hearse in Quincy. Has been deputy sheriff of Branch county for three years and is still holding that position. Is the owner of some fine stock consisting of stallions and brood mares. Has a good property in Quincy. January 8, 1894, he associated himself with Mr. Barlow in the purchase of the Commercial Livery and Sales Stables and together with this gentleman is running the stables.

Hildebrand, Fred, farmer of Algansee township, is a native of Germany, born September 1, 1839. He came to this country in 1860, and came directly to Quincy. He worked by the month on a farm for two years and then rented a farm for a period of three years, at the expiration of which period he purchased his present farm of one hundred and forty-six acres on sections 13 and 16. He is very pleasantly located, having a nice home and farm buildings, enjoying in his declining years the fruits of his energy and pluck. In 1867 he was married to Charlotte Hageman, who came from Prussia when nineteen years of age. To this union were born one son now living at home, and one daughter who is the wife of Thomas Goodman in Algansee township. Mr. Hildebrand is a member of the Detective Horsemen's Association of Branch county. Has held the office of treasurer two full terms, also has been a member of the Board of Review.

Hilton, T. A., "The Best Clothier" and men's furnisher of Coldwater, came from England when a boy direct to this city. Beginning at the bottom of the ladder in a grocery store he soon began to make his mark, and by steady habits and self-perseverance climbed its full length, during which time he took up special branches of study and finished them later on with much credit to himself. After one year as station agent at Fremont, Ind., on the Fort Wayne branch he retired, and came back to Coldwater as clerk in grocery, which position he filled until the situation of accountant was tendered him by Mr. L. D. Halsted in the clothing and fur trade, who at the end of one year gave him charge of his entire business, which Mr. Hilton managed successfully for five years, and resigned to become a partner under the firm of Moises Bros & Hilton, which partnership expired at the end of four years by limitation, when Mr. Hilton withdrew, and soon thereafter embarked and prudently managed a business of a like nature for himself. Continuing in this line for about six years, his health began to fail and forced him to retire. After closing out his stock and a few months' rest, the opportunity presented itself to purchase the clothing, hat and furnishings from Messrs. McPherson & Sons, which he has conducted for several years and is now the largest of its kind in the county, his trade extending over Branch and adjoining counties. Mr. Hilton has served the city in an official capacity with honor, and is prominent in many orders and societies for the promotion of good, and is held in high esteem as a public-spirited citizen.

Himebaugh, Noah. One of the well known farmers of Noble township is the subject of this sketch, Mr. Noah Himebaugh. He is the son of Daniel Himebaugh, a native of Niagara county, N. Y. His father was one of the pioneers of Branch county, having become a resident of the county in 1835, and resided there until his death of September 4, 1892. Our subject was married at the age of thirty-three years to Miss Melissa Miller. This union was blest by one son Elmore, who was born February 12, 1870. His wife died on December 11, 1880. Mr. Himebaugh has been a resident of Branch county during nearly his entire life, and for fifty-six years has resided on the farm he now owns. He has been successful as a farmer and his genial manner has won for him many warm friends.

Holcomb, Nattie, Mrs., resident of Coldwater, was born in Branch county in 1847. Her school days were spent in the schools of Coldwater. In the year 1868 she was married to Walter Cornell, and to them was born one child, Myrtie, still living. In the year 1875 Mr. Cornell died and in 1880 the subject of this sketch was married to Horace Holcomb. To this second union has been born two sons, Roscoe and Roy. Mrs. Holcomb is an active member of the Methodist church of Coldwater.

Hollister, A. N., farmer of Mattison township, is one of the leading men of his vicinity. Is owner of a fine farm which he moved onto in 1868, and which he now has under a high state of cultivation and improved with fine buildings. In 1881 he was elected justice of the peace and is a member of Eagle Lodge No. 124, F. & A. M. at Burr Oak.

Holmes, C. J., is one of Branch county's leading farmers who owns a fine farm of seven hundred and twenty-seven acres a short distance west of the village of Bronson. Also sixty acres within the limits of village. Mr. Holmes was born and reared on the farm where he now resides, which is well improved and upon which he has a fine home and four excellent tenant buildings.

Houck, W. J., a member of the Board of Supervisors of Branch county, is a native of that county, having been born on the farm where he now resides in Algansee township. His parents have been residents of Branch county since 1839. His father, William Houck, was a native of New York, but died here in 1869. Our subject, Mr. W. J. Houck, was educated in this county and has been engaged in farming during his entire life. His first duty as public official was that of township clerk, serving from 1884 to 1891. In 1893 he was elected Supervisor for Algansee township and is now filling that office. He is a general farmer and his farm is well adapted to grain and stock raising, the wheat yield being from 18 to 25 bushels to the acre, and corn from 35 to 70 bushels per acre. Mr. Houck's service as a county official has been very satisfactory to the public in general, and he enjoys the distinction of being the youngest member of the Board of Supervisors.

Howard, G. W., a resident of Coldwater township, was born in Albany county, New York, August 25, 1836. He came to Branch county in 1857 and worked at his trade of carpenter until March, 1862, when he enlisted in company K, 9th Michigan Cavalry, and served until the close of the war of the rebellion, since which time he has been engaged in farming, giving special attention to stock culture. He has made improvements to the amount of $3,500 and is now one of the thrifty farmers of the county. Mr. Howard is a trusted counselor by his many friends in important business transactions, as well as a good educator with the permanent class of his community.

Howe & Legg, attorneys and counsellors-at-law. The firm consists of Charles F. Howe and Charles N. Legg, organized January 1, 1893, both members having practiced their profession previous to that time. Charles N. Legg, the senior member of the firm and probate judge of the county, is a native of New York. Mr. Legg was elected probate judge in November, 1892, for four years, now serving this term. He also held the office of prosecuting attorney from 1880 to 1885. Has served as circuit court commissioner and member of the school board. Is interested in the banking interests of the county. Charles F. Howe, junior member of the firm, is a native of Lancaster, Ohio. Was educated in Washington city and the schools of Coldwater. He began the study of law under Judge Legg, and was admitted to the bar in November, 1889, practicing his profession alone until this partnership was formed in 1893. They are successful in their line and are doing a large paying business.

Hoyt, M. R., a prosperous farmer of Bethel township, is a native of New York state, having been born there in 1831. At the age of fifteen he became a resident of Angola, Indiana, and continued to reside there for twelve years. In 1859 he was united in marriage to Josephine Hoffman, and in the same year removed to Gilead, Michigan. In 1890 he again moved and became a resident of Bethel township. His father, Rufus Hoyt, was born in Connecticut in 1815 and when a mere boy moved to New York with his parents, where he afterwards married Caroline Potter, the mother of our subject. His father died on December 30, 1888, aged sixty-three years. His mother is still living. Mr. Hoyt is one of the successful farmers of Bethel township, and is well and favorably known throughout the county.

Humphrey, L. F., attorney-at-law, of Coldwater, is a native of the state of Indiana. He began the study of law in 1883 in the office of William E. Ware, of Coldwater, and later with Barlow & Loveridge. Was admitted to the bar April 16, 1885, and has practiced continuously in Coldwater since that time, having been quite successful and is building up a well paying practice.

Hunt, M. L., resident of Quincy, was born at Waterloo, Ind., and moved from there to Jackson county, Michigan, and later to Branch county. Was

court commissioner for four years, and filled several township offices. He conducts a general law business and also an insurance agency at Quincy. He has been successful in the practice of his chosen profession and is one of the rising young attorneys of Branch county.

Long, James, M. D., is the oldest practising physician of Coldwater. He is a native of New York city. He received his earlier education in Woodstock, Vt. After completing his literary course he began the study of medicine in the year 1849. He completed his medical education by a course in the medical department of the university of New York, graduating therefrom in the year 1852. He followed the practice of his profession in the city of New York for five years. He came to Michigan in 1857, locating in Detroit. In the year 1862 he came to Coldwater where he has since resided, being in active practice all of the time, and is considered one of the leading physicians in southern Michigan.

Loveridge, Hon. Noah P., present circuit judge of Branch and St. Joseph counties, Mich., was born in New Milford, Litchfield county, Conn., in 1826. He received a common school and academic education in the schools of that county, residing there until he was twenty-one years of age. He next taught school for some time in New Jersey, and while doing so studied law at Morristown, in that state. In 1850 and 1851 he attended the Fowler law school at Ballston Spa, N. Y., and in the autumn of 1851 entered the law office of Judge William E. Curtis, 106 Broadway, New York. In March, 1852, he was admitted to the bar at the city of Brooklyn, and the following year commenced the practice of law at Cuba, N. Y., where he remained until 1866. He then removed to Coldwater, Mich., and associated himself with the Hon. John B. Shipman. Later on he formed a partnership with H. H. Barlow, Esq., which partnership existed until May, 1882, when he entered the law bureau of the interior department at Washington, D. C., under Hon. Henry M. Teller, secretary of the interior, and while there was engaged in writing opinions relating to the public lands, and continued in that work until 1884, when he was appointed deputy commissioner of pensions by President Arthur, filling that office during Mr. Arthur's administration. In May, 1885, he returned to Coldwater, and in the following year visited the Pacific coast. In autumn of 1886, with his family visited Europe, where he remained a year. During his absence in the spring of 1887 he was elected judge of the 15th judicial circuit. He entered upon the duties of this office January 1, 1888, and continued until January 1, 1894, when he resumed the practice at Coldwater with his son Henry C. Loveridge. Judge Loveridge is considered one of the ablest judges in Michigan, and his service in that capacity has reflected great credit and honor on himself.

Loveridge, Henry C., attorney-at-law, Coldwater, Mich., was born in Cuba, N. Y., in 1858, and moved with his father's family to Coldwater, Mich., in 1866. He was educated first in the Coldwater high school, graduating from there in 1874, after which he taught school for two years. In 1876 he entered Trinity college, at Hartford, Conn., graduating from there in 1880. He soon after entered the law office of Loveridge & Barlow, and remained there until his admission to the bar in 1882. After his admission to the bar he associated himself with H. H. Barlow in the practice of law, under the firm name of Barlow & Loveridge. This partnership existed until the fall of 1887, since which time he has been alone. Mr. Loveridge has been a success in the past in the practice of his profession, and is now one of the leaders of his profession in Branch county.

Lowery, Jefferson, farmer of Sherwood, was born and raised in Matteson township. Is the owner of one hundred and thirty-two acres of farm land within the corporate limits of the village of Sherwood, most of it being under cultivation, well adapted to raising of grains of all kinds and live stock.

Lucas, Joseph L., farmer, Quincy township, came to Adrian, Mich., in 1837. He purchased the land on which he now resides in 1838 from Ira S. Mudge and moved onto it in March, 1839, and resided there ever since. The house in which he now lives is the old original frame, gradually improved and added to, having never moved. He was married in the same house in 1847, to Phebe Coon, who died November 25, 1890. He has four daughters and two sons living and four children dead. Has held several township offices and positions of responsibility. Has been engaged in the nursery business and in buying stock and wheat. Had contract for erecting the first warehouse for the R. R. company.

Luce, Cyrus G., was born in Windsor, Ashtabula county, Ohio, July 2, 1824. In 1836 he came with his parents to Orland, Steuben county, Indiana. As a boy he went to school in the proverbial log school-house of the day during three winter terms, afterwards attending the Collegiate Institute at Ontario, Ind., for three terms. At the age of seventeen he commenced work in his father's wool-carding and cloth dressing establishment, located on Crooked Creek, two miles east of Orland. He worked in and had the general charge of the shop for seven years. At the age of twenty-four he became the owner of eighty acres in Gilead, Branch county. In August, 1849, he was married to Julia A. Dickinson, of Gilead and resided on the farm where they commenced, until August, 1882, when the wife of his youth was called hence. Five children were born to them, four of whom are still living. He was again married in 1883 to Mary E. Thompson, of Bronson. In 1852 he was elected supervisor of his township, and was subsequently re-elected on ten different dates, serving eleven years. In the year 1854 he was elected to the legislature. In 1858 and again in 1860 he was elected county treasurer. In 1864 and 1866 he was elected to the state senate. In 1867 was elected a member of the constitutional convention held that year. In 1879 he was appointed state oil inspector by Governor Croswell, serving in the position three and one-half years. In 1884 his name was presented to the republican convention and strongly pressed as a nominee for governor, but he was defeated by a majority of thirty by General Alger. In 1886 he was nominated for governor by acclamation and elected by double the majority given two years before. In 1888 he was renominated as the unanimous choice of the convention. During his active life he has received twenty nominations for office and every one of these has come to him by acclamation. At the session of the legislature in 1893 he had many strong friends among the members and a host of them all over the state who desired his election to the United States Senate. Farming has from the year 1848 to the present time been his main business. He has taken a deep interest in the development of his town, county, state and country. For twenty years has been very earnest and active in his efforts to stimulate the ambition of his fellow farmers.

Luce, Emery G., resident of the township of Gilead, was born in the same township February 14, 1852. He is the son of ex-Governor Luce. Has resided upon section 16 since the year 1876, which he has improved to the highest stage of cultivation, having a home which is a model in all respects. His barns and other buildings are of the best character. He has served the people as township treasurer and highway commissioner for several years. He pays considerable attention to stock culture.

Luedders, E. D., Coldwater, has the principal boot and shoe store of the city. The business was founded by Mr. Luedders in 1877. He is a native of Germany, coming to America when thirteen years of age, living with his parents in the city of Cincinnati where he learned the trade of shoemaker. He came to Michigan in 1865 and located in Coldwater where he followed his trade until 1877 when he opened a shoe store upon a small scale, which he has gradually increased until he now has the largest as well as the best selected stock of boots and shoes in the county. He is a stockholder in the Branch county savings bank which he assisted to organize. He has been successful in business and is well known throughout the county. His city residence is at 146 West Chicago street.

Mabrey, S. Curtis. The subject of this mention, Mr. S. Curtis Mabrey, was born in Otsego township, Steuben county, Indiana, in the year 1865, and at ten years of age moved with his parents to Gilead township, Branch county, where Mr. Mabrey grew to manhood, receiving his education in the schools of that county. In January, 1888, he was united in marriage to Miss Alice Cheney, of Ovid township and to this union came one son, H. Clare Mabrey, born October 19, 1889. Mrs. Mabrey departed this life in 1892. Mr. Mabrey's parents were Silas and Mary A. Mabrey, who were married in 1849, and who were residents of Steuben county, Indiana for some twenty-eight years. Mrs. Mabrey's parents were Reuben and Mary Cheney, of Ovid township, who came from England at an early day.

MacDonough, Thomas, resident of Coldwater township, came to the place where he now resides, two miles east of the city of Coldwater, from Cheboygan, Mich., in October, 1892, where he had formerly been engaged in lumber and general merchandise business. He is now living a retired life.

MacDonough, Thompson, son of the above gentleman and residing with him, is engaged in the business of breeding high-grade and trotting horses. Although Mr. MacDonough has been in this county but a short time, he has already established a reputation as an owner and judge of horses and doubtless will, in the near future, be rated as one of the foremost horsemen in this county. He is a lover of horses and takes much pleasure in training them. The farm and buildings are admirably adapted to the business that Mr. MacDonough has chosen. The home and the buildings are very attractive and beautifully surrounded by a grove of finely developed maple trees.

McDougal, J. W., farmer, residing upon section 12, Bethel township, was born in Crawford county, Ohio, in 1846. When he was three years old his parents died. When six years of age he was taken by his uncle, John Robertson, of Medina county, Ohio, with whom he made his home until, at the age of sixteen, he joined the army of the Union in the rebellion, enlisting in the 129th Reg. Ohio Vol. Infantry. After serving eight months he returned home, but after an interval of sixteen days, he re-enlisted in the 25th Reg. Ohio Vol. Light Artillery and served until close of the war. He was married in the year 1871 to Miss Genevra Walker of Branch county, daughter of Josiah and Jane Walker, who emigrated from England in 1836, and to this union three children have been born, two daughters and one son. Mr. McDougal has a farm of seventy-one acres, with an excellent home and fine improvements.

McCrary, Clay, farmer and stock-raiser of Sherwood, is a native of the same township, and has always resided in Branch county, excepting a few years spent in the west. His farm of two hundred and forty acres upon which he now resides, is mostly improved and is but a few miles from the place of his birth. This town, in which his boyhood days were spent, he still considers to be the finest spot on earth.

McKenzie & Hyslop, proprietors of the Quincy Roller Mills, which they purchased in the year 1857. Their average daily output is one hundred barrels of flour, their special brand being the "Pride of Quincy," which has a wide reputation and is shipped to all points in the country. Theirs is one of the solid business firms of Branch county. Mr. McKenzie is a native of Williamstown, W. Va. Mr. Hyslop came to Quincy from South Allen, Mich., and was former proprietor of the mills at that place for thirteen years.

McVay, E., farmer, resident of Butler township, was born in Clovis, Ohio, October 1, 1851, where he lived until twenty years of age, when he came to Branch county, living at Quincy for some years. He has been successful as a farmer and is comfortably situated.

Mallach, Walter, Quincy, farmer, was born in Hanover, Jackson county, Mich., September 24, 1847, where he lived on a farm until 1858, when he moved to the town of Pulaski, and attended school at that place. Was married in the year 1875 to Kate L. Scrimer of Pulaski. He moved from Jackson into Hillsdale county, where he bought a farm, remained six years, then sold out and came to Branch county in 1883, and bought a farm of one hundred and twenty acres on section 9, Quincy township, where he now resides.

Mallow, George W., resident of Bronson township, engaged in general farming business and raising of stock. He owns a farm of one hundred and twenty acres two miles southwest of Bronson, where he has lived since 1879. Is a member of the F. & A. M. society.

Mallow, J. J., farmer and stock raiser of Sherwood, came from St. Joseph county, Mich., in 1850, settling on the farm where he now resides. He owns one hundred and thirteen acres of good land, most of which is under cultivation; has good modern house and barns.

Mann, Peter J., farmer, residing upon section 22, Girard township, is one of the representative farmers of the county, where he has resided for the past fifty-eight years.

Maple Park Stock Farm, founded by Mr. A. C. Fisk in 1852. Mr. Fisk is a native of the state of New York, born near Rochester, came to Branch county in 1835, settled in Coldwater and purchased part of his present farm east of the city in the same year. In the early part of 1852 he purchased Green Mountain Black Hawk, a trotting bred stallion, and was the first trotting bred horse ever brought into the state of Michigan. This horse afterwards went to Louisville, Ky. Since that time Mr. Fisk has

Members of Branch County Bar.

1 Judge N. P. Loveridge
2 Hon. Chas. Upson (deceased)
3 Ex Judge John B. Shipman
4 Ex Probate Judge Norman A. Reynolds
5 Ex Probate Judge Charles N. Legg
6 Charles E. Champion
7 Milo

8   Melvin E. Peters
9   Clayton L. Johnston
10 Elmer E. Fisher
11 Wm. H. Compton, Pros. Att'y
12 H. H. Barlow
13 John R. Champion
14 Caleb D. Randall

15 Henry C. Loveridge
16 Hadley M. Wells
17 Frank O. Newberry
18 A. B. Kimball
19 Wm. H. Lanckerts
20 M. A. Auldfield
21 Charles F. Howe

BRANCH COUNTY SAVINGS BANK, COLDWATER, MICH.
Incorporated under the Laws of Michigan.
PAYS 3 PER CENT. ON DEPOSITS.

PORTRAIT AND RESIDENCE OF GEORGE STARR, COLDWATER, MICH.

RESIDENCE OF H. H. SMITH, BETHEL TOWNSHIP.

FRIEDMAN & CO., QUINCY, MICH.

THE BEARDSLEY STOCK FARM,
BRONSON TOWNSHIP, BRANCH CO., MICH.

offices of his township. Is a man well known and highly respected for his integrity. Is a member of the Free Methodist church.

Tift, E. V., farmer, residing on section 2, Gilead township, was born in the same township in the year 1863, where he has continuously resided since. Was married in 1890, to Miss Sadie A. Richardson, of Bronson, Mich., and they have since resided upon their homestead, having a fine farm under the highest stage of cultivation, well improved in all respects. Mr. Stephen Tift, the father of the subject of this sketch, is a native of Allegany county, N. Y. where he was born in the year 1823. At the age of ten years he moved with his parents to Washtenaw county, Mich., and three years later to Branch county. Rebecca Trisch was born in Stark county, Ohio, moved to Dekalb county, Ind., in 1856, was married to Stephen Tift in 1862, and came to Branch county at that time.

Treat, Egbert W., one of the leading farmers of the county, is a native of Branch county, his father settling in the township of Ovid in the year 1837. The subject of this sketch grew to manhood in the same township where he now owns three hundred and seventy-two acres of land. He has given particular attention to the breeding of short-horned cattle, and has a fine herd of over twenty head. He is now engaged in the handling of the Spellmyer wire fence, and has applied for a patent on one of his own inventions. Has also been engaged in buying and shipping lumber to some extent. He has served as justice of the peace in Ovid township, also school inspector, and has taken some interest in general politics. He has been successful and is considered one of the leading men of the county. Is a stockholder in the Branch County Savings Bank. Has resided in the city of Coldwater since 1890.

Trump, G. W., farmer, residing on section 30, Coldwater township, moved there from Ovid township in 1879. He settled in Ovid township in 1866, where he resided until his removal as above. His parents and grandparents settled in Starke county, Ohio, in an early day, emigrating there from a point near Philadelphia, Pa. Mr. Trump is engaged as general farmer, having an excellent reputation and is respected by all who know him.

Tucker, C. M., genial proprietor of the farmers feed barn and livery, is one of the best known men in Union City. He was born in St. Lawrence county, N. Y., on September 26, 1833. Came to Michigan when seventeen years of age, and was engaged in milling in Calhoun county for several years. He afterwards moved to Wisconsin, but again returned to Michigan. In 1892 he began the livery and feed business and has made a decided success of the same. Mr. Tucker is now alone in the world, his wife and child having both died in about 1882. He is well-known over the county, and enjoys a good business.

Tuttle, Timothy, farmer, residing in Kinderhook township, was born in Syracuse, N. Y., in the year 1832, coming west in childhood with his parents, who settled in Marshall county, Ind., where he resided until the age of twenty-two, when he moved to Branch county where he has resided ever since. He was married in the year 1853, and located on section 19, Kinderhook township.

Umsted, William, farmer, residing in Gilead township, was born in Bethel township, Branch county, in 1843, residing there until 1871, when he moved to the farm he now occupies on section 6 which he has improved to the highest stage of cultivation. He pays some attention to the breeding of draft horses of the best kind. His farm consists of three hundred and sixty-seven acres of the finest land in the county, upon which he has made a beautiful home for himself.

Upson, Hon. Charles. The subject of this mention was born in Southington, Conn., March 19, 1821, and died at Coldwater, Mich., September 6, 1885. He attended the district school of his native town until his thirteenth year, when he entered the select school of Jesse Olney, the compiler of Olney's series of Geographies. He then entered the academy of his native town which he attended for two winters, after that he taught for seven winters, two of which he was in charge of the schools in Farmington, Conn. He next was a student in the higher academical course at Meriden, Conn. In the spring of 1844, he began the study of law with Judge Lowry, at Southington, and in the fall of the same year entered the Yale college law school, remaining there one year. In the fall of 1845 he removed to Michigan, teaching in Constantine, St. Joseph county, the following winter. In 1846, he entered the law office of Gurney & Hammond, at Centerville, and in January, the following year, was appointed deputy clerk of St. Joseph county, and was admitted to the bar the same year after being examined before the supreme court at Kalamazoo. He served two years as deputy clerk, and in 1848 was elected county clerk, which position he held for two years. In 1852 he was elected prosecuting attorney for St. Joseph county and filled that office for two years, at the end of which time he was nominated and elected state senator from that county. In 1856 Mr. Upson moved to Coldwater and formed a partnership with the Hon. George A. Coe, forming the law firm of Coe & Upson. In 1857 was appointed a member of the railroad commissioners and served as such for four years. In 1860 was nominated by the republican party as a candidate for attorney general of the state, to which office he was elected. In 1862 he was elected representative to congress, and was re-elected in 1864, and again in 1866, serving in all three terms. In the spring of 1869 Mr. Upson was elected judge of the 15th judicial district which office he held until December 31, 1872. In 1871 he was appointed by Governor Baldwin as one of two commissioners to examine the compilation of the laws made that year. In 1873 he was appointed by Governor Bagley as one of the commissioners who met in Lansing to revise the constitution and report amendments thereto. In 1880 he was elected state senator from St. Joseph and Branch counties by a handsome majority. In 1883 he was defeated in the republican state convention for justice of the supreme court. During his life Mr. Upson served the city of Coldwater as its mayor, and was also a member of its school-board. In 1865 he assisted in the organization of the Coldwater national bank. Was married August 3, 1852, to Miss Sophia Montgomery Upham, and was the father of three children.

Van Aken Bros., livery, feed and sale stables, hack and wagonette line, Coldwater. The business was founded by J. H. Van Aken in 1866, and conducted by him until 1887, when Mark J. and Bernie L., his sons, purchased the business and have since enlarged it to more than twice its original capacity, making it one of the most extensive and completely equipped establishments of its kind in southern Michigan. They keep an average of twenty first-class driving horses and have an exceptionally fine assortment of carriages, buggies and hacks, also two elegantly appointed and finished funeral cars. Both these gentlemen are natives of Branch county, and are well and favorably known. By long and extensive experience they have acquired a thorough knowledge of the livery business, which makes them eminently well qualified to successfully manage such an establishment, their patrons, therefore, always being sure of courteous treatment and satisfactory service. Mr. M. J. Van Aken is a member of the city council, having represented the first ward in that body for four years. Mr. B. L. Van Aken is a popular and prominent member of the local Masonic and K. P. lodges.

Vanaken, George W., resident of Coldwater, is a native of Monroe county, N. Y. He came to Michigan in the year 1835, settled in Lenawee county, living there until 1836, when he removed to Girard township, and engaged in farming, which he followed until about one year ago. For the past seven years he has engaged in buying and shipping live stock. He has given considerable attention to breeding and raising fine horses. George W., record 2:20, was raised by him. Of late years he has given some attention to raising sheep. He has served as supervisor of Girard township for fourteen years, and in 1871 and 1873 served in the state legislature. He is a stockholder and director in the Branch County Savings Bank.

Van Fleet, A. S., Bronson, dealer in grain, farm produce and poultry, successor to W. H. Gibson & Co., who established the business in 1888. Mr. Van Fleet succeeded to the business in October, 1892. He is one of the prominent men of Bronson and has filled numerous places of honor. He was for a number of years a member of the firm of H. Powers & Co., general merchants. He has resided in the village thirty-one years and is known as an active, energetic business man.

VanNuys, Jacob H., farmer, residing in Matteson township, was born in Seneca county, N. Y., in the year 1841. Moved with his parents to Lenawee county, Mich., when nine years of age, and two years later moved to Branch county. Has been a farmer resident of Michigan all his life except five years, during which he was engaged as farmer in Steuben county, Ind. He settled on the farm now occupied by him in the year 1881. He served nine months in 1865 as a soldier in Company H, 11th Michigan Infantry, in the war of the rebellion.

Victory, Jackson L., farmer, residing in Butler township, was born in Lenawee county, Mich., April 18, 1844. His parents moved to Butler township in the year 1853. February 2, 1863, Mr. Victory enlisted in the union army, joining the First Regiment, Michigan Light Art., and served until the close of the war. He was mustered into the service at Coldwater April 11, 1863, and left for the front May 20, going to Kentucky. Went into his first action with his command at Triplet Bridge, Ky., June 16, 1863, and was with the battery in all of its engagements, including the Morgan raid during that year. Went into winter quarters at Cumberland Gap, Tenn., December 12, 1863, and was stationed in the fortification there until June 29, 1864, when his command was again furnished with horses and went to Knoxville, arriving there July 1. There he was assigned to the Second Brigade, Reserve Artillery, 4th Division, 23d army corps, and continued on service at Knoxville until December 8. With one section and twenty-five men was detached and ordered to Strawberry Plains, Tenn., to guard a railroad bridge over Halsteen River at that point. On the 8th of January, 1865, he was taken sick and sent back to Knoxville where he remained in his tent about three weeks. On the 31st of January, he was sent to the hospital at Knoxville and remained there until May 25, when he was transferred to Nashville, Tenn., staying there until July 5, when his brother from the north came after him, obtained a furlough for him and brought him home, where he remained until September 6, 1865, when he was mustered out of the service at Detroit, Mich. While in the service with the battery he participated in the engagements at Triplet Bridge, Ky., June 16, 1863, at Lebanon, Ky., July 5, 1863, at Buffington Island, Ohio, July 19, 1863, Steubenville, Ohio, July 26, 1863; Loudon Bridge, Tenn., September 22, 1863. In the army record, his name appears as Vickory instead of Victory, his correct civil name. He is a member of Col. Loomis Post No. 2, G. A. R. and U. V. U. of Coldwater. He was married to Emeline Crandall, who was a native of Litchfield, Mich., May 6, 1866.

Wakeman, M. B., register of deeds, Branch county, was born in the state of Ohio and came with his parents to Branch county when a child. He grew to manhood in this county, and for many years conducted a grist-mill and saw-mill in Algansee township. He served the people four years as township treasurer, eight years as supervisor, and in 1892 was elected to the office of register of deeds and is now serving his first term as such.

Walker, Charles A., Bronson, livery stables, established business in 1886, near the depot. In 1889 he purchased the business of T. J. Ferguson, in the rear of Clark House. He is the leading man in that business, in fact, has the best stable in the county outside of the city of Coldwater. He was appointed deputy sheriff in January, 1891, and is now filling his second term as such, having been a very successful officer, making as many important arrests during his incumbency as any officer in the county. As an officer and as a business man he is well and favorably known, possessing pluck and energy to be successful in anything he undertakes.

Wattles, M. K. The subject of this mention, M. K. Wattles, is one of the representative men of Branch county. He is a native of New York, but became a resident of Michigan in 1863, locating in Kalamazoo, and for five years filled the responsible position of division superintendent of the Lake Shore and Michigan Southern Railway for the Grand Rapids division. Prior to accepting this position Mr. Wattles was engaged for fifteen years by this company, and also filled the position of superintendent of construction for the Nickel Plate Railroad, personally superintending the work on that line between Chicago and Fort Wayne, Ind. He was also connected with the Rock Island Road for two years as superintendent of the southwest division of Kansas extension on that system. In the winter of 1890 Mr. Wattles became a resident of Coldwater, and at the present time is engaged in farming. Since becoming a resident of Branch county he has taken an active interest in county politics and is now president of the Farmers' Alliance of the county. He has also been interested in the banking institutions of the county and for one year had the management of the bank of Sherwood. He is at present a stockholder in the Branch county savings bank. The success that attended his efforts in railroad circles has followed him in other lines of business.

Weaver, Allen, farmer, residing upon section 2, Gilead township, has one of the best farms in the county, consisting of one hundred and twenty acres under the highest stage of cultivation. For the past ten years the average yield of wheat upon his farm

.

Official Register

OF BRANCH COUNTY, MICHIGAN.

Showing County and Court Officers, and Years of Service of Each.

COUNTY CLERKS.

Wales Adams, served from 1833 to 1836
C. F. West, " 1836 to 1840
M. B. Sullivan, " 1840 to 1844
C. P. Benton, " 1844 to 1846
S. E. Ross, " 1846 to 1850
P. P. Wright, " 1850 to 1854
E. O. Leach, " 1854 to 1856
B. C. Webb, " 1856 to 1862
H. N. Lawrence, " 1862 to 1866
F. M. Bissell, " 1866 to 1874
F. D. Newberry, " 1874 to 1880
J. B. Dickey, " 1880 to 1892
E. A. Greenamyer, " 1892

COUNTY COMMISSIONERS.

C. G. Hammond, served 1835 to 1839
Elon G. Berry, " "
Wales Adams, " "
Enos G. Berry, " 1840
Wales Adams, " "
Hiram Shoulder, " "
Wales Adams, " 1841
Hiram Shoulder, " "
Oliver D. Colvin, " "
Hiram Shoulder, " 1842
Oliver D. Colvin, " "
Hiram Gardner, " "

COUNTY SEAT COMMISSIONERS.

Geo. Trapp, served 1837 to 1850
Jonathan Holmes, " "
Jas. B. Tompkins, " "
Daniel Wilson, served 1850 to 1850
Admaius Shaw, " "
A. R. Day, " "
J. B. Southworth, served 1850 to 1851
A. R. Day, " "
Thom Croft, " "
H. Cary, served 1861 to 1862
A. R. Day, " "
J. B. Southworth, " "
A. R. Day, served 1862 to 1863
H. Haynes, " "
H. Cary, " "
H. Haynes, served 1863 to 1864
A. R. Day, " "
H. Wilson, " "
H. Haynes, served 1864 to 1868
J. O. Fulton, " "
A. R. Day, " "
J. R. Bennett, served 1868 to 1871
G. W. Fisk, " 1871 to 1873
W. J. Barnes, " 1885 to 1887
A. F. Azelne, " 1887 to 1893

STATE SENATORS.

Sam'l Etheridge, Coldwater, 1839-1841
H. A. Warren, Coldwater, 1841-1843
G. A. Coe, Coldwater, 1845-1847
H. G. Berry, Quincy, 1847-1849
A. French, Bronson, 1850-1852
J. C. Leonard, Union, 1852-1854
C. P. N. Wilson, Coldwater, 1856-1858
Asahel Brown, Coldwater, 1858-1860
Darius Monroe, Bronson, 1860-1864
C. G. Luce, Gilead, 1864-1866
J. B. Jones, Quincy, 1868-1870

C. D. Randall, Coldwater, 1870-1872
J. H. McGowan, Coldwater, 1872-1874
J. H. Jones, Quincy, 1874-1876
F. F. Morgan, Coldwater, 1876-1878
J. W. French, Sherwood, 1878-1880
Chas. Upson, Coldwater, 1880-1893
Ezra L. Koon, Hillsdale, 1882-1884
G. A. Smith, Somerset, 1884-1886
Ferry Mayo, Battle Creek, 1886-1888
Alfred Milnes, Coldwater, 1888-1892
Marden Sabin, Centerville, 1893-18—

SHERIFFS.

Wm. McCarty, served 1833 to 1836
J. B. Stewart, " 1836 to 1838
J. H. Stevens, " 1838 to 1847
Amelia Arnold, " 1845 to 1846
Hiram Shoulder, " 1846 to 1848
James Pierson, " 1848 to 1850
Philo Porter, " 1850 to 1854
Daniel Wilson, " 1854 to 1856
D. N. Green, " 1856 to 1860
John Whitcomb, " 1860 to 1864
Chas. Powers, " 1864 to 1866
L. M. King, " 1866 to 1870
B. B. Johnson, " 1870 to 1874
J. T. Culp, " 1874 to 1878
L. Wilson, " 1878 to 1882
O. C. Campbell, " 1882 to 1886
A. T. Kinney, " 1886 to 1890
H. Sweet, " 1890 to 1894

PROSECUTING ATTORNEYS.

Eaton G. Fuller, served 1837 to 1843
H. C. Gilbert, " 1843 to 1849
E. G. Parsons, " 1849 to 1850
J. W. Gilbert, " 1850 to 1852
J. G. Parkhurst, " 1852 to 1854
J. W. Turner, " 1854 to 1856
E. N. Nichols, " 1856 to 1862
L. T. N. Miller, " 1862 to 1864
G. A. Coe, " 1864 to 1866
W. W. Barrett, " 1866 to 1868
J. N. McGowan, " 1868 to 1872
F. L. Sketch, " 1872 to 1874
B. B. Kitchell, " 1874 to 1880
C. N. Legg, " 1880 to 1884
J. B. Champion, " 1884 to 1886
W. E. Wars, " 1886 to 1889
E. E. Palmer, " 1889 to 1892
W. H. Compton, " 1892

CIRCUIT COURT COMMISSIONERS.

E. G. Fuller, served 1850 to 1825
J. G. Parkhurst, " "
Justin Lawyer, " 1852 to 1855
J. B. Clark, " 1856 to 1858
W. W. Barrett, " 1858 to 1862
David Thompson, " 1862 to 1864
F. E. Morgan, " 1864 to 1866
W. J. Bowen, " "
J. H. McGowan, " 1866 to 1868
W. J. Bowen, " "
A. M. Tinker, " 1868 to 1870
J. Bowen, " "
F. A. Sketch, " "
Ezra Berry, " 1873 to 1873
C. D. Wright, " 1873 to 1876
Ezra Berry, " "

C. D. Wright, served 1876 to 1878
A. N. Legg, " "
N. A. Reynolds, " 1876 to 1880
C. N. Legg, " "
M. D. Campbell, " 1880 to 1882
A. J. McGowan, " "
M. D. Campbell, " 1882 to 1884
F. D. Newberry, " "
F. D. Newberry, " 1884 to 1886
D. M. Wells, " "
D. M. Wells, " 1886 to 1888
F. A. Lyon, " "
H. O. Viets, " 1888 to 1892
W. H. Lockerby, " "
C. G. Johnson, " 1892 to 18—
M. D. Folsom, " "

CORONERS (since 1854).

Isaac Middaugh, served 1854 to 1856
Israel B. Hall, " "
A. C. Fisk, " 1856 to 1858
C. D. Brown, " "
J. N. Bennett, " 1858 to 1860
C. D. Brown, " "
G. W. Johnson, " 1860 to 1862
Elmer Parker, " "
Warren Byrne, " 1862 to 1864
Elmer Parker, " "
Daniel Miller, " 1864 to 1866
J. C. Hall, " "
Moses E. Chauncey, " 1866 to 1868
Barnabas Shawcroft, " "
J. R. Bennett, " 1868 to 1870
G. W. Johnson, " "
J. S. Wolcott, " 1870 to 1872
N. Tetterly, " "
C. H. Lovewell, " 1872 to 1874
Jacob Kincaid, " "
C. H. Lovewell, " 1874 to 1876
Edward Purdy, " "
Jerome Wolcott, " 1876 to 1878
A. A. Van Orthwick, " "
Roland Root, " 1878 to 1880
D. J. Sprague, " "
D. J. Sprague, " 1880 to 1884
A. B. Burrows, " "
A. Burrows, " 1884 to 1886
A. W. Barber, " "
A. W. Barber, " 1886 to 1888
J. H. Montague, " "
A. W. Barber, " 1888 to 1890
J. A. Montague, " "
J. H. Montague, " 1890 to 1892
G. D. Galen, " "
J. H. Montague, " 1892 to 18—
W. R. Card, " "

REGISTERS OF DEEDS.

Seth Dunham, served 1833 to 1838
Leonard Ellsworth, " 1838 to 1843
Jared Pond, " 1843 to 1846
Sidock Seymour, " 1846 to 1850
Albert L. Porter, " 1850 to 1854
Carlis H. Youngs, " 1854 to 1858
Francis B. Way, " 1858 to 1862
Francis T. Eddy, " 1858 to 1862
Phineas F. Nichols, " 1867 to 1866
Charles A. Edmonds, " 1868 to 1870

Daniel A. Douglas, served 1870 to 1874
Franklin T. Eddy, " 1874 to 1876
William H. Donaldson, " 1876 to 1880
Zelotes G. Osborn, " 1880 to 1886
Geo. H. Turner, " 1886 to 1892
Mortimer B. Wakeman, " 1892 to —

REPRESENTATIVES IN LEGISLATURE.

Hiram Alden, Coldwater, 1835-1837
W. A. Kent, Bronson, 1838-1839
Jared Pond, Branch, 1839-1839
C. G. Hammond, Union, 1839-1841
Juston Goodwin, Union, 1841-1843
Martin Olds, Batavia, 1842-1843
Wales Adams, Bronson, 1843-1845
W. B. Sprague, Coldwater, 1845-1846
Alvarado Brown, Quincy, 1845-1847
Justin Goodwin, Union, 1846-1847
Alvarado Brown, Quincy, 1847-1848
B. F. Ferris, Sherwood, 1847-1848
Geo. A. Coe, Coldwater, 1848-1849
O. D. Culver, Kinderhook, 1849-1850
Roland Root, Coldwater, 1849-1850
S. L. Lawrence, Girard, 1850-1852
Roland Root, Coldwater, 1850-1852
W. H. Arnold, Quincy, 1852-1854
B. F. Tompkins, Girard, 1852-1854
C. G. Luce, Gilead, 1854-1856
H. C. Hurd, Union, 1854-1856
Ralph Leland, Quincy, 1855-1856
Edward Perry, Union, 1856-1858
A. S. Glovener, Coldwater, 1856-1860
Edward Perry, Union, 1858-1860
Wm. Chase, Kinderhook, 1860-1862
H. C. Hurd, Union, 1860-1862
Jesse Bowen, Quincy, 1862-1864
C. W. Wetherby, Gilead, 1862-1864
Amos Smith, Girard, 1862-1864
M. Haynes, Coldwater, 1864-1866
J. H. Jones, Quincy, 1864-1866
D. Monroe, Bronson, 1864-1866
J. S. Barlow, Coldwater, 1866-1868
J. D. Neall, Sherwood, 1866-1868
J. H. Jones, Quincy, 1866-1868
I. D. Neall, Sherwood, 1866-1870
E. Bushwick, Union, 1868-1870
J. A. Williams, Quincy, 1868-1870
J. A. Williams, Quincy, 1870-1872
M. Haynes, Coldwater, 1870-1872
G. F. Gillam, Bronson, 1870-1872
G. W. Van Aken, Coldwater, 1872-1874
E. J. Welker, Kinderhook, 1872-1874
G. F. Robinson, Noble, 1874-1876
G. W. Van Aken, Coldwater, 1874-1876
H. J. Welker, Kinderhook, 1876-1878
R. K. Teasdall, Quincy, 1876-1878
C. T. Thorpe, Sherwood, 1878-1880
J. R. Bennett, Coldwater, 1880-1882
J. D. Easton, Union City, 1880-1882
D. J. Easton, Union City, 1882-1884
E. Himebaugh, Bronson, 1882-1884
M. D. Campbell, Coldwater, 1884-1886
Amos Gardner, Coldwater, 1884-1888
A. A. Van Orthwick, Butler, 1888-1890
D. D. Buell, Union, 1890-1892
D. D. Buell, Union, 1892-18—

MEMBERS OF CONSTITUTIONAL CONVENTIONS.

Harry Warner, Coldwater, Sept. 1836

J. D. Tompkins,   Gorand,   Dec. 1838
Wales Adams,   Bronson,   —— 1850
Alvarado Brown,   Quincy,   —— 1850
Amihai Brown,   Algansee,   —— 1850
Cyrus G. Luce,   Goland,   —— 1867
Amihai Brown,   Coldwater,   —— 1867

COUNTY JUDGES

Peter Marvin,   served 1833 to 1837
Martin Olds,   "   1837 to 1840
Edward A. Warner,   "   1841 to 1842
Wm. B. Sprague,   "   1843 to 1844
Esbon G. Fuller,   "   1844 to 1848
Harvey Warner,   "   1849 to 1850
Jonathan H. Gray,   "   1850 to 1860
Welson D. Shrole,   "   1860 to 1864
David Thompson,   "   1864 to 1868
David S. Green,   "   1868 to 1881
Norman A. Reynolds   "   1881 to 1893
Chas. N. Legg,   "   1893 to ——

COUNTY SURVEYORS (since 1854)

P. M. Sprague,   served 1854 to 1856
Murray Knowles,   "   1856 to 1860
S. H. Eye,   "   1860 to 1862

A. B. Day,   served 1862 to 1866
N. S. Andrews,   "   1866 to 1870
Titus Babcock,   "   1870 to 1872
J. H. Bennett,   "   1872 to 1876
Murray Knowles,   "   1876 to 1880
Charles Hamilton,   "   1880 to 1886
N. L. Knowles,   "   1886 to 1888
J. H. Bennett,   "   1888 to 1891
I. P. Miner,   "   1891 to 1892
A. Q. Bushnell,   "   1892 to ——

COMMISSIONERS OF COMMON SCHOOLS.

W. S. Perry,   served 1867 to 1869
A. A. Jones,   "   1869 to 1871
A. A. Luce,   "   1871 to 1873
M. D. Campbell,   "   1873 to 1875

COMMISSIONERS OF COUNTY SCHOOLS.

S. S. Stafford,   served 1887 to 1890
D. W. Herman,   "   1890 to 1893
D. A. Teller,   "   1893 to ——

JUDGES OF CIRCUIT COURT.

P. N. Smith,   served 1854 to 1866
N. Bacon,   "   1866 to 1870

C. Upson,   served 1870 to Feb. 1873
S. W. Melendy,   "   Feb. to June 1873 to 1873
C. B. Brown,   "   June to Mar. 1873 to 1874
E. W. Keightley,   "   Mar. to Jan. 1874 to 1877
David Thompson,   "   Jan. to Dec. 1877 to 1879
J. B. Shipman,   "   Dec. 1878 to 1881
Russell B. Fenler,   "   1882 to 1869
Noah P. Loveridge,   "   1886 to 1894

ASSOCIATE JUDGES OF CIRCUIT COURT.

S. A. Holbrook,   served 1833 to 1836
W. A. Keel,   "   1833 to 1836
W. B. Sprague,   "   1837 to 1838
C. G. Hammond,   "   1837 to 1840
E. G. Berry,   "   1839 to 1840
W. A. Keel,   "   1841 to 1844
Martin Barnhart,   "   1841 to 1846
Island K. Hard,   "   1846 to 1846

COUNTY JUDGES AND SECOND JUDGES.

W. A. Keel, county judge, 1847 to 1850
Jacob Shook, second judge, 1847 to 1850
Josiah Sawyer, county judge, 1851 to ——
Darwin Littlefield, second judge, 1851

COUNTY TREASURERS.

Seth Dunham,   served 1833 to 1840
J. G. Corbus,   "   1840 to 1842
J. T. Haynes,   "   1842 to 1850
H. R. Alden,   "   1850 to 1853
Wales Adams,   "   1853 to 1854
Horace Shoudler,   "   1854 to 1858
C. G. Luce,   "   1858 to 1864
M. V. Calkins,   "   1862 to 1866
John Wisdom,   "   1866 to 1872
L. P. Wilcox,   "   1872 to 1876
J. R. Dorkey,   "   1876 to 1880
E. W. Beaton,   "   1880 to 1884
D. F. Tich,   "   1884 to 1888
B. B. Gorman,   "   1888 to 1899
J. B. Meuler,   "   1899 to ——

County Officials.

1. Charles N. Legg, Probate Judge
2. Hezekiah Sweet, Sheriff
3. M. B. Wakeman, Regt. of Deeds   4. E. A. Grossmeyer, County Clerk
5. James D. Mosher, County Treasurer   6. W. H. Cureton, Pros. Attorney

Directory

OF

RESIDENTS AND FREEHOLDERS

OF BRANCH COUNTY, MICHIGAN.

BATAVIA TOWNSHIP

Angevine, S. C., Cold Water.
Austin, H. C., Batavia Station.
Abramson, Frank, Olds.
Bowers, John, Cold Water.
Bates, Samuel,
Burrell, Aaron, Olds.
Beard, A. E., "
Burch, Verne, "
Burch, Lee, Quincy.
Donnell, Adaline, Batavia Station.
Donnell, Homer, "
Donnell, Mrs. G. H., "
Boys, Richard, "
Burch, Admiral, Olds.
Bullock, Pergalia, "
Burch, Austin, "
Burch, A. L., "
Bolton, Burton, Olds and Cold Water.
Blackwell G. W., Cold Water
Bailey, S. G., "
Barnhart, Frank, Olds.
Bolton, J. F., "
Bergdoll, Albert, Bronson.
Bowers, L. H., Cold Water.
Bates, Chas., Batavia Station.
Burch, Lyon, Olds.
Bates, F. N., Batavia Station.
Buffham, H. F., "
Brock, Edward, "
Bowerman, L. L., "
Brasi, Henry, "
Brown, M. W., Cold Water
Brown, Ed., "
Burch, Mrs. E., Olds.
Bergloff, Fred, Bronson.
Burch, Austin, Olds.
Blood, Frank, Batavia Station.
Card, W. B., "
Cleveland, Howard, Cold Water.
Crist, John, "
Crist, H. A., "
Cleave, Ambrose, Batavia Station.
Cole, S. B., Coldwater
Campbell, James, Coldwater
Crawford, W. B., Olds
Crawford, F., Olds
Corson, L. W., Matteson
Cooley, A. W., Coldwater
Cleveland, G. W., Coldwater
Corey, B. W., Union City
Card, James, Batavia Station
Crandall, James, Olds
Card, W. S., Batavia Station
Dufue, John, Union City
Drumm, Chas., Batavia Station
Davey, Wm. Jr., Coldwater
Dorsey, Jesse, Batavia Station
Daybroth, Jacob, Olds
Davey, Wm., Sr., Coldwater
Daybroth, Frank, Olds
Drumm, Elecro, Batavia Station
Drumm, Sylvester, Batavia Station
Drumm, Morris, Batavia Station
Drake, Julia A., Batavia Station
Drumley, Mrs. L. D., Batavia Station
Daw, R. W., Bronson
Ensley, Jacob, Coldwater
Ensley, James, Coldwater

Ensley, Lydia, Olds
Elliott, W. W., Batavia Station
Fletcher, B M., Coldwater
Fry, Fred, Coldwater
Fikine, Mark, Olds
Field, Chas., Olds
Fiat, Seymour, Olds
Fry, Mrs. C. D., Coldwater
Fry, Edgar, Coldwater
Fairbanks, S. D., Coldwater
Fairbanks, Frank, Coldwater
Fonda, W. B., Coldwater
Fonda, C. I., Coldwater
Fox, A. G., Olds
Fredbother, John, Bronson
Foster, J D., Bronson
Fletcher, H. E., Coldwater
Fry, Johnson, Coldwater
Foster, Wm., Bronson
Filmer, D. W., Olds
Gowdy, L., Coldwater
Green, Elijah, Olds
Gosiny, Gref, Coldwater
Gnew, A. B. Coldwater
Greene, Ward, Coldwater
Greener, A., Coldwater
Green, L., Coldwater
Galen, d. P., Olds
Gillagie, Jesse, Olds
Grayce, Floyd, Olds
Gallupg, Albert, Coldwater
Gray, J. M., Coldwater
Galluge, Leroy, Coldwater
Gallupg, Frank, Coldwater
Gifford, Ira, Batavia Station
Gifford, Edward, Batavia Station
Gifford, Giles, Batavia Station
Gaul, O. W., Coldwater
Graf, Chas., Batavia Station
Gillagie, Wm., Olds
Hill, A. C., Coldwater
Haehng, B., Matteson
Hurley, Leonas, Olds
Hopkinson, C. T., Matteson
Hurley Wm., Olds
Hawley, L. L., Olds
Richard, L. P., Olds
Herrill, Julius, Coldwater
Harva, Perry, Olds
Hubbard, S. C., Union City
Hastie, F. A., Olds
Hashing, J. W., Matteson
Harkness, R. D., Batavia Station
Hanks, L. W., Coldwater
Hastings, Jno., Olds
Hawley, D. T., Olds
Hawley, John, Olds
Hurley, Allen, Olds
Harris, Simon E., Batavia Station
Hubbard, Leroy, Union City
Hurley, Adelbert, Olds
Hayt, W. N., Coldwater
Hosley, Harry, Olds
Hadley, Allie, Olds
Ide, Henry, Coldwater
Isabar, James, Coldwater
Ide, Amelia, Coldwater
Ide, Stevens, Olds
Johnson, A. P., Matteson

Johnson, Sara, Matteson
Jones, C. N., Olds
Jones, Frank, Bronson
Jordan, E. M., Olds
Kintes, Geo., Bronson
Kintes, Eugene, Bronson
Knowles, D. A., Olds
Kimbell, Elizabeth, Union City
Kimball, H. F. & Wm., Union City
Kimbell, H. L., Union City
Kline, Jennie, Olds
Khan, Fred, Olds
Kerr, Coldwater, Coldwater
Kibalaskie, Andrew, Bronson
Kibalaskie, Eleven, Bronson
Lewis, B. E., Coldwater
Larew, D. S. P., Olds
Lake, Wm., Olds
Mitchell, B. L., Union
Miller, H. D., Olds
Morrison, Mr. R., Coldwater
Moss, Nelson, Olds
Martin, Ira, Coldwater
Martin, J. R., Coldwater
Masat, John, Olds
Manser, Frank, Olds
Mitchell, Mary, Union City
Mitchell, Ansell, Union City
Mitchell, Carrie, Union City
Miller, H. H., Olds
Miller, Geo., Olds
Miller, W. H., Olds
Moore, H. C., Olds
Miller, W. A., Olds
Mooreliman, W. H., Olds
Moore, Warren, Olds
Mills, Rachel, Bronson
Moore, Frank, Olds
Moore, Mrs. Chas., Olds
Murphy, James, Batavia Station
Mangrus, Peter, Olds
McMaster, G. A., Batavia Station
Murphy, J. A., Batavia Station
Murphy, J. B., Batavia Station
Mowry, Wm., Batavia Station
Noyes, G. P., Coldwater
Noyes, Mary A., Coldwater
Noyes, Austin, Coldwater
Noyes, Lydia, Coldwater
Noyes, E. J., Coldwater
Olmstead, M. E., Batavia Station
Olmstead, Benj., Batavia Station
Olds, M. P., Olds
Olds, C. L., Olds
Powlinke, Geo., Bronson
Pond, P. M. Batavia Station
Phelps, Geo., Coldwater
Paddock, Loren, Olds
Pikine, Philip, Olds
Pitcher, P. H., Olds
Pierre, L. E., Coldwater
Peterson, James, Coldwater
Peterson, E. J., Coldwater
Paine, Thos. Jr., Bronson
Paine, Thos. Sr., Bronson
Paine, M. H., Bronson
Pierce, Chas., Coldwater
Perrin, Martin, Batavia Station
Perrin, Mrs. D. J., Batavia Station

Plumb, Wm. Batavia Station
Reid, David, Coldwater
Richard, J. A., Olds
Reynolds, Jamse, Olds
Rachenge, Geo., Bronson
Russell, Asa, Coldwater
Ryder, N. F., Olds
Reynolds, Alfred, Olds
Reeding, Thos., Batavia Station
Reeding, John, Batavia Station
Smith, G. W., Batavia Station
Stoneman, J. B., Batavia Station
Stoneman, M. P., Batavia Station
Stoneman, J. W., Batavia Station
Stoneman, J. H., Batavia Station
Sheets, Abn, Batavia Station
Sixberry, Alonzo, Matteson
Bugstat, John, Bronson
Scribner, J. H. & F., Bronson
Stone, John, Batavia Station
Stone, Irvine, Batavia Station
Stratton, John, Batavia Station
Shaw, Geo., Batavia Station
Shelden, Leroy, Union City
Salisberry, Clark, Olds
Schmults, Mrs. Tobius, Batavia Station
Seeley, John, Olds
Stephen, J. T., Olds
Simmonds, C. W., Batavia Station
Schurtz, John, Batavia Station
Smith, Sam'l, Batavia Station
Sayles, Nelson, Olds
Sayles, Orvis, Olds
Saulsberry, Chas., Olds
Tyler, A., Union City
Tolib, Mrs. L., Bronson
Teitle, G. A., Matteson
Taylor, Mrs. Jas., Batavia Station
Taylor, Leonard, Bronson
Taylor, Watson, Bronson
Taylor, John, Bronson
Taylor, S. F., Bronson
Teller, Theron, Olds
Tyler, W. M., Olds
Tuttle, Mrs. L. R., Batavia Station
Trumbull, Sylvester, Union City
Trumbull, Chas., Union City
Vanderhoff, O. A., Olds
Vandteers, Chas., Batavia Station
Willis, Geo., Olds
Willis, G. E., Olds
Willis, Wm., Olds
Webbe, Chas., Olds
Webb, Fred, Olds
Waters, L., Bronson
Wright, John, Olds
Workington, Carrie, Olds
Wilcox, Jed, Coldwater
Wilcox, David, Olds
Woodard, Chas., Batavia Station
Watze, Wm., Olds
Wagner, Geo., Olds
Wilcox, Albert, Olds
Worden, J. L., Matteson
Welch, Wm., Bronson
Wilcox, Elvin, Olds

KINLAN TOWNSHIP

Austin, J B., Butler.
Russell, M. A., Fazon.

CITY OF COLDWATER.

Whitnall, Belle L.
Wells, D. M.
Wells, J. B., Sr.
Wells, J. B. Jr.
Wheelen, Geo. H.
Wilcox, W. B.
Williams, Clarence A.
Whitehead, Frank
Woodward, H. J. & Son
Waite & Walker
Ward, Mary C.
Wheeler, R. C.
Wolcott, J. S.
Walker, A. B. & Co.
Whitnall, L. B.
Warren, Mrs. Chas.
Watkins, Helen S.
Weller, Winifred
Wilhams, C. H.
Wakeman, M. R.
Wolcott, Mrs. Elizabeth
Webb, Mrs. B. L.
White, David
Whitman, Wm.
Whitehead, Mrs. Jas.
Whitelock, Thos C.
Waite, G. W.
Woodmaster, Henry
Wongin, Spencer W.
Wish, Mrs. Mollie
Ward, Wm.
Walcott, C. S.
Wood, J. D.
Williams, F. N.
Williams, D. C.
Woodward, H. J.
Wilder, Mrs R. M.
Williams, S. P.
Warner, Dr. C. D.
Warmie, Mrs. Kate
Warren, John
Welters, Mrs. Elizabeth
Warren, Lou
Williams, S. M.
Whitaker, Miss Lizzie
Wilson, Mrs R. S.
Whitehead, F. B.
Walker, Wm.
Woodson, Dr. C. H.
Wilson, Gustine
Waffle, Wm.
Wilson, Judadiah
Whitten, Geo. Mrs.
Williams, R. H.
Wilcox, Ed.
Williams, Geo.
Warren & Dallister
Warner & Son
Wilson, Perry
Warren, J. H. D.
White, G. A.
Whitehead, G. W.
Whitley, Ellen C.
Whitley, H. C.
Weller, Winnie
Williams, Harlow
Williams, W. J.
Worden, D. B.
Whitford, Eliza
Whedon, Eugene
Weiz, Homer
Warner, Ray
Wixon, H. C.
Whalen, Edward
Wilcoit, H. A., Mrs.
Wood, Hiram
Walcott, E. A.
Williams, Effie
Walker, Thos.
Walker, James
Williams, Mrs. S.
Wright, Fred
Wheeler, Milan
Warren, F. A.
White, Wm.
Yapp, Clarence, Mrs.
Young, Eveline
Young, H. N.
Yapp, C. T.

Youngs, Mrs. Anna
Zeller, Wm.
Zeller, Stephen & Harriett
Zeller, Chas.
Zeller, Frances
Zorn, Lorin

CALIFORNIA TOWNSHIP.

Ayres, E. J.
Anstey, Chas.
Broughton, E. H.
Bates, A. W.
Bascom, D. T.
Bascom, Norman
Bertrum, John
Bail, Uriah
Bassage, Alford
Cass, I. A.
Copland, J. H.
Carrns, B. M.
Copland, Armonia
Colvin & Lethridge
Carithers, Kate
Chestnut, Sam'l
Chestnut, Margret
Clark, Barney
Chessmuth, Nettie
Chestnut, R. J., Jr.
Cleveland, A. A.
Carlton, John
Crago, G. M.
Dunlap, James
Dunlap, John
Dunlap, Elvan
Doyle, Tobo., Sr.
Doyle, John, Jr.
Duty, C. M.
Duty, Mrs. A. B.
Duty, Almira K.
Dufer, E. L.
Dawson, Sybil
Ellis, W. T.
Ellis, D. L.
Ellis, R. J.
Enard, M. L.
Eshinaw, Sam'l
Flynn Brothers
Fishbender, I. C.
Filley, Oliver
Gibson, P. D.
Gibson, D. J.
Goodrich, Wm.
Graham, E. W.
George, J. B.
Greer, June
Graham, Otella
Goodwin, Wm.
Goodwin, Fred.
Harrington, Ellis
Holsfdyen, Geo.
Hotchkiss, Sara
Hall, Hanna
Hake, John
Harris, Alex.
Hagerman, J. L.
Hania, Geo.
Jeffers, G. W.
Kelso, Henry
Kirkland, A. S.
Lawrence, J. R.
Lannsby, Wm.
McMorray, Hugh
Miller, G. P.
McLeoith Chas.
Norton, R. J.
Odron, Albert
Paul, Jane E.
Paul, W. L.
Paul, Milan
Pridgeon, Abram
Pridgeon, John
Pemly, Abigal
Patinson, W. L.
Quackenboush, Geo.
Reed, Jennie
Speer, David
Speer, T. J.
Speer, Jas.
Sharer, David
Sharer, Sam'l
Sharer, Wm.

Sharer, Albert
Stockdale Henry
Stockdale Ben.
Skinner, M. D.
Stallings, Wm.
Talmadge, Wm.
Toall, Oliver
Trosman, David
Vance, Alex.
Vance, A. B.
Vanettan, Dan'l
Woodward Bethona
Wilkinson S. F.
Wilkinson, Adalbert
Wilson, Abigal
Ward, Fremont

SHERWOOD TOWNSHIP.

Annis, G. W., Sherwood
Alger, Dillard,
Anstes, Miss M. A., Sherwood
Baad, Geo.,
Barton, Lafayette,
Bathrick, Lyman,
Beall, Harrison,
Beall, Arthur,
Billings, D. L., Union City
Borth, Wm., Sherwood
Blossom, Emery, Sherwood
Bnerl, I. J., Athens
Blackman, Isabel, Sherwood
Beard, Columbus,
Bullison, King, Sr.,
Bennett, Frank,
Bascom, Thos.,
Bascom, Flora,
Boshang, John, Albans
Bailey, Smith, Sherwood
Blossom, Winnie, Colon
Beckwith, Mrs. Orpha, Sherwood
Bennett, Spencer,
Banker, John A.,
Bartlett, Arthur,
Beall, G. W., Union City
Bethrick, O. S., Sherwood
Bole, Edward,
Bennell, Bert Mrs.,
Barton, James,
Boshang, Jamie, Athens
Bethrick, Chas., Sherwood
Bennett, J. F.,
Corbin, S. B., Union
Chptell, P. J., Colon
Cole, H. L., Sherwood
Carswell, Edward, Sherwood
Campf, Jerome,
Collins, J. G.,
Coddington, Salona,
Cline, S. A.,
Cross, Argalus A.,
Cole, Elsworth,
Crocker, C. A.,
Calvers, A. B.,
Chrominski, Joe.,
Carswell, Elliot,
Chireman, W. B.,
Doubleday, H. S.,
Danks, J. S., Union
Davis, S. D., Sherwood
Davis, W. T., Mrs., Sherwood
Davis, H. E.,
Dofer, L. S.,
Drabews, Anson,
Darfoe, D., Athens
Dane, Joseph, Sherwood
Dane, M. C., Colon
Dane, Harvey,
Doubleday, H. M., Sherwood
Dore, Henry,
Drouk, Sam'l,
Dorsey, Mary A.,
Dashen, J. C., Union
Drabro, D. B.,
Davis, J. J., Sherwood
Davis, James, Union
Dennole, Celinda, Sherwood
Ensign, Alex A.,
Engle, Eugene, Athens
Favorette, Richard, Athens
Fredenburgh, M F
French, F. E., Sherwood

Fox, John P., Athens
Fulton, Marah C., Factoryville
Failing, C. B., Sherwood
Failing, Caroline,
Prager, C. A., Union
Fouple, J. B., Sherwood
Franly, S. P.,
Francisco, Geo.,
Fraser, Robert,
French Bros.,
French, J. W.,
Fulton, G. W.,
Favorette, Adam, Athens
Farrand, Joseph, Colon
Fasner, W. R., Sherwood
Griffis, Hiram, Athens
Gidner, J. F.,
Griswold, A. H., Union City
Gwin, John, Sherwood
Gwin, E. J.,
Gaine, Jesse,
Goodrich, James, Colon
Gillespie, Sarah, Sherwood
Gwin, James,
Gordon, R.,
Gaine, W. W.,
Gillespie Elsworth, Sherwood
Greenfield, E. D., Athens
Ghering, Alford, Sherwood
Haveland, J. B., Athens
Harrington, A. J., Union City
Howard, E. B. Sherwood
Hall, Chas.,
Hibner, A. A.,
Haas, J. B.,
Haler J. M.,
Haler, S. L., Colon
Herman, John, Union City
Hanes, R. B., Sherwood
Hemingway, N. B.,
Hills, A. L.,
Maganbargh, C. G.,
Hanes, M. C.,
Hanes, Earl,
Huntley, Truman,
Hicks, Wm.,
Hanes, E. L.,
Henry Warren,
Hannah, W. E.,
Hanson, Wm.,
Henry Julius,
Hawthorne, Luthera, Mrs., Athens
Hodge, F. A., Sherwood
Hill E. R.,
Huntley, Geo.,
Jones, Clark,
Jones, J. D.,
Jones, H J.,
Jones, Bauhen,
Jones, John,
Jones, S. A.,
Jackson, Richard,
Jackovich, Martin,
Jones, M. C.,
Jackson, C. L.,
Kloes, A. B.,
Kilbourn, Charlott, Union City
Kilbourn, Halton, Sherwood
Kimber, R. E.,
Kent, D. W.,
Kellogg, C. D., Athens
Kellogg, Orsampon,
Kilbourn, R. L., Sherwood
Kinyon, Merrik, Athens
Kirby, Y. B.,
Kirby Chas.,
Kirby, Chester,
Kidney, Henry, Sherwood
Ketchum, Nat., Athens
Kissell, Noah. Sherwood
Kissell, Chas., Sherwood
Kotosh, Simon, Athens
Latham, G. D.,
Lee, William,
Lehr, Milton B., Athens
Leatharberry, Finlay, Sherwood
Leatharberry, C. S. L.,
Lake, C. C., Union City
Lowry, Jefferson, Sherwood
Locke, Melissa,

SHERWOOD TOWNSHIP.

Locke, G. F., Sherwood
Locke, Mrs R. I., "
Locke, P. J., "
Lyon, Amanda A., "
Lilly, Mary A., "
Lackent, Wesley, "
Laird, Mrs. Van., "
Lee, Horton A., "
Lincoln, R. H., Union
Lovejoy, Lucius, Sherwood
Larkin, Andrew, "
Luther, Curtis, Union
Locke, James M., Sherwood
Lyon, J. D., "
Long, R. S., "
Liebard, Frank, Athens
Leatherberry, Elmer, Sherwood
Leatherberry, Mahlon "
Mead, Mrs., Colon
McIntyre, J. T., Sherwood
Mallen, J. J., Union
Mason, C. A., Sherwood
Mallary, Clay, "
Maure, Mrs. Sara, Sherwood
Mound, Jacob, "
McCarey, Frank, Union City
McCarey, Leroy, "
McCarty, Dan'l, Sherwood
Mitchell, Eugene, "
Milligan, Nat, "
MiniteD, Geo., "
Milligan, N. & H., "
Millet, A. B. "
Mowry, Henry, "
Merrill, D. L., "
Malcom, Judson, "
Meyer, Fred. "
Meacham, A. M. "
Nearing, Wm., "
Nowaski, John, "
Narbor, Coleman, "
Nearing, Alva C., "
Nallthorp, Louisa, "
Olmstead, Porter, Union
Olds, Orlando, "
O'Bryan, J. T., Sherwood
Osborn, L. B., "
Osborn, Geo., "
Pierce, O. L., "
Pierce, Frank, "
Putman, C. M., Union
Pride, F. C., Sherwood
Peck, H. S., Union
Parsons, Soloman, Union City
Prentis, Charlott, Sherwood
Pierce, L. J., "
Powlss, Selah, "
Rathbone, C. D., "
Rathbone, P. J., "
Reton, Peter, Athens
Rider, Matilda, Union
Robinson, C. L., Sherwood
Robinson, R. M., "
Robinson, Lorena "
Robbins, C. L., "
Rumsey, Dan'l, "
Richards, Jacob, Sr., "
Russell, W. H., Athens
Russell, J. T., "
Runyan, Henry, Sherwood
Rench, Reuben, Union
Rench, Sam'l "
Richards, Jacob, Jr., Sherwood
Reton, Andrew, "
Shreer, Buran, "
Shaw, John, "
Rumsey, Chas. "
Rider, R. B., "
Simons, Rodney, Athens
Simons, S. J., "
Stanton, W. A., Union
Standard, James, Athens
Spencer, Wilson, Sherwood
Shaw, Sam'l, Union
Slagert, Wm., Athens
Smith, M. E., Sherwood
Spencer, A. F., "
Sherwood, N. A., "
Smith, H. D., Union

Stanton, Edward, Sherwood
Stay, Isaac, "
Selby, W. M. "
Smith, Elnora, "
Sparlock, B., "
Savin, Isaac, "
Savin, M. E. Mrs., "
Swan, C. E., "
Sargent, Edmond, "
Sayres, Carrie "
Sayres, Mrs. C., "
Shaw, Justin, "
Stafford, Amelia "
Stadley, John. "
Stadley, Emeline "
Spencer, James, "
Skinner, James, "
Spencer, M. A., "
Shonnugroth, Marky, Athens
Saylor, A. J., Sherwood
Smith, Wm., "
Stanton, John. "
Scarping, Jno., "
Seymore, G. H., "
Turner, W. W., Sherwood
Thurlow, W. C., "
Thurlow, Lafayette, Matteson
Thurston, M. F., Sherwood
Thayer, Sarah "
Thayer, Jacob, "
Taylor, Fred "
Tiffany, Jeremiah, "
Thurston, R. K., "
Thayer, Jackson, "
Travante, R. M., Mrs., "
Thayer, W. & J., "
Travante, L., "
Thayer, Wm., "
Thayer, Anna "
Thayer, John, Mrs., "
Taylor, R. B. "
Vanhorne, H. L., "
Vreeland, F. N., "
Washburn, Eliget. "
Wolfe, Presley, "
Watkins, Anna Mrs., Union
Watkins, Viol, Sherwood
Wilson, Newcomb, "
Wells, J. E., "
Wrigglesworth, J. J., "
Wells, Wm., "
Wilson, W. W., "
Woodruff, Isaac, Union
Wilcot, Dan'l, Sherwood
Watkins, Z. W., "
Watkins, L. A., "
Watkins, Marian, "
Wilks, Chris. "
Wilcot, L. F. "
White, Margaret, "
Webb, Joseph, "
Wrigglesworth, Wm., "
Wells, Perry, Athens
Watkins, Caroline, Sherwood
Wilson, B. C., "
Watson, L. F., "
Wolfe, Nancy "
Zimmerman, L.

GIRARD.

Abel, M. T., Tekonsha.
Ackerly, M. C., Girard.
Adams, W. H., Coldwater.
Achlicks, Henry, "
Adolph, Augustu, "
Adolph, Philip, Hodunk.
Aldrich, A. J., Coldwater.
Aldrich, L. D., Girard.
Algoe, S. R., "
Allen, Chas., "
Anderson, J. H., "
Anson, Julian, Coldwater.
Anson, Warkworth, Union City.
Baird, H. P., Hodunk.
Bailey, G. W., Girard.
Bailey, Jas., "
Bailey, Chas., "
Barney, Jas., "
Barney, A. C., "
Barcom, W. A., Coldwater.
Barry Samuel, Hodunk.

Bartlett, J. G., Tekonsha.
Bartlett, Henry, "
Bacon, Ed., Girard.
Ballard, T. F., "
Bassett, A. J., Hodunk.
Bassett, D. C., "
Bisson, H. H., Coldwater.
Bickford, G. A., Girard.
Bidwell, S. D., "
Birch, Lucinda, Coldwater.
Bishop, Jas., Girard.
Bowers, J. S., "
Brewster, Geo., Coldwater.
Brown, David, Hodunk.
Brown, A. R., Coldwater.
Brooks, Robt., "
Brooker, Mary, Girard.
Bush, J. J., Coldwater.
Byronki, Jno., Hodunk.
Calkins, C. W., "
Carpenter, S. A., Tekonsha.
Carter, Wm., "
Caris, H. K., Girard.
Cathertown, H., "
Chancey, A. J., Coldwater.
Chaney, M. E., Mrs., Union City.
Chickering, W. H., Coldwater.
Chordavoine, Robt., Girard.
Clement, C., Coldwater.
Clement, J. H., "
Cook, H. M., Girard.
Comstock, Henry, Hodunk.
Corey, Q., Coldwater.
Corey, Albert, Girard.
Cowell, Reuben, Coldwater.
Cowell, Chauncy, Union City.
Cowes, W. J., Girard.
Cox, Frank "
Craig, Elias, Hodunk.
Cudner, Homer, Coldwater.
Curtiss, Charlott "
Davis, J. H., Tekonsha.
Davis, J. E., "
Daykin, Cordelia, Girard.
Derling, Frank, Tekonsha.
Dayton, Enier, Girard.
Dean, Ed, "
Dean, Leonard, "
Dedrick, J. E., "
Dembrook, C., "
Demorest, Wm., "
Demorest, Theodore, "
Demorest, C. F., "
Dewey, Sally, "
Dice, Selina C., "
Dohenik, Joseph, Coldwater.
Doolittle, F. W., Tekonsha.
Dutcher, J. M., Coldwater.
Duke, M. W., Girard.
Devering, Joel, Tekonsha.
Eberhard, Emma, Union City.
Edwards, Arthur, Girard.
Eldridge, C. H., Tekonsha.
Eldridge, G. H., "
Eldred, A. D., "
Eldred, J. E., "
Elling, Theron, "
Elling, Frank, "
Ellon, J. M., Girard.
Estes, L. R., Tekonsha.
Everitt, Daniel, Girard.
Everitt, Phena, "
Farwell, Frank, "
Foster, W. S., "
Foster, Reuben, "
Fox, David, "
Fox, Frank, "
Fox, Lyman, "
French, John, Union City.
French, E. K., Union City.
Fry, E. F., Coldwater.
Fulcher, G. H., Coldwater.
Geer, Roy, Girard.
Gillett, G. S., "
Gorball, C. F., Girard.
Gardner, Amara, "
Gorball, Mary, "
Gordon, Edd., Tekonsha.

Gould, C. K. Coldwater.
Gould Bros., "
Gould, Alvira, "
Granger, John, "
Granger, A. J. Girard.
Greeley, John, Coldwater.
Greenwood, Geo., Coldwater.
Grove, J. P., Hodunk.
Grobosh, Mike, Union City.
Gruner Bros., Coldwater.
Goff, Fred, Tekonsha.
Hall, Alfred, Girard.
Hamon, Nancy, Hodunk.
Hartley, Frank, Tekonsha.
Hartly, C. E., "
Hawley, W. S., Coldwater.
Hayes, Henry, "
Hiddle, Thos., "
Hills, J. C., Hodunk.
Hollenbeck, R. D., Girard.
Hollenbeck, F., Coldwater.
Hollenbeck, C. G., Girard.
Hollenbeck, C. M., "
Hubbard, P. A., Union City.
Hudson, Mary, Girard.
Hogmire, David, Coldwater.
Hurst, R. R., Girard.
Hurd, W. H., Coldwater.
Hunker, Geo., "
Hunker, H., "
Hutchinson, C. S., Coldwater.
Ingleeby, S., Girard.
Jackman, J. F., "
Johnson, P. C., "
Johnson, G. W., "
Johnson, C. L., "
Johnson, G. B., "
Kapinski, Jno., Union City.
Keep, Sara, Coldwater.
King Bros., Girard.
Kingsley Bros., Girard.
Kingston L., "
Kingston, Dan'l, Hodunk.
Koans, Sara, Girard.
Krause, C. S., Union City.
Knapp, Chas., Tekonsha.
Kosrinski, Thos., Union City.
Lake, M. A., Girard.
Lake, W. W., Girard.
Lake, Ann E., Girard.
La Doe, Ed., Girard.
Langwell, W. H., Coldwater.
Lawrence, S. K., Girard.
Lee, C. C., Coldwater.
Leggett, H., "
Leismring, H., "
Lewis, J. Z., "
Leadenker, Sally, Girard.
Leonin, Adna, "
Loomis, Warren, "
Lering, G. K., "
Loring, Sanford, "
Leasing, W. H., Coldwater.
Lutes, S. M., Girard.
Lynner, Edson, "
Mack, T. C., Hodunk.
Major, John, Girard.
Mann, P. Q., "
Mann, Mark, "
Mark, Jay, Hodunk.
Manu, J. W., Girard.
Mann, Geo., "
Manchester, L., Tekonsha.
Markham, A., Coldwater.
Markham, Mark, "
Miller, Patience, Girard.
Morford, Phoebe, Coldwater.
Morford, J. B., "
Morrison, P. P., "
Morrison, A., "
Musser, J. C., Girard.
Niverson, W. K., Coldwater.
Nye, L. L., Girard.
Odson, Alex., Coldwater.
Olney, Wm., Girard.
Olney, Henry, "
Orton, J. H., "
Ostron, R. C., "
Ostrom, L. D., "

Greene, Anthony, Coldwater
Good, Solomon, "
Graves, A. B., "
Granger, Francis, "
Good, James, "
Good, Walter, "
Gregory, Bert, "
Griffin, C. K., "
Gillett, J. F., "
Gilbert, Cyrus, "
Grimley, Erastus, "
Gleason, A. S., "
Gregor, M. A., "
Gardner, L.D.&C.J., "
Haynes, Harvey, "
Haynes, Levi, "
Hill, Homer, "
Hill, Albert, "
Hill, J. L., "
Hand, C. A., "
Howe, A. B., "
Harmon, Reuben, "
Harmon, G. H., "
Hunt, B. B., "
Howard, G. W., "
Howe, G. E., "
Houghtaling, Frank, "
Hilliar, C. E., "
Hale, P. O., "
Holcomb, Mrs. Nettie, "
Howland, Willis, "
Henning, Albert, "
Hillier, P. M., "
Hoffman, John, "
Howland, Rev. B., "
Henry, Thos. J. "
Jeffords, Mrs. R. B. "
Joseph, S. S. "
Jackson, G. W. "
Kobe, Alma E. "
Keeley, Michael "
King, Wm. "
Knowlen, Andrew "
Kempster, Stephen. "
Legg, A. H. "
Lockwood, Rufus "
Lockwood, Mrs. Sara "
Lockwood, Jeremiah "
Lockwood, Herbert "
Lewis, J. J. "
Lewis, Harriet C. "
Lowe, Geo. W. "
Leek, A. J. "
Lynd, Mrs. Permelia "
Legg, Edward "
Lyman, R. B. "
Lewis, J. N. "
Lake, Bruno "
Lehr, Mrs. Chas. "
Leaf, Joshua "
Loveridge, Clare "
Lewis, N. B. "
Luckett, Charles "
Leomen, F. C. "
Modlert, Matthew "
Moore, Robt. "
Milton, C. H. "
Murphy, James "
Moore, A. F. "
Messenger, Jerome "
Martin, J. G. "
Matthew, G. B. "
Magley, Wm. H. "
Miller, Geo. "
Miller, Edwin "
Mason, G. C. "
Markoff, Fred "
Merritt, Daniel "
Morford, J. S. "
Munn, Mrs. W. H. "
Newman, Wm. "
Newman, Stephen "
Norton, W. P. "
Nye, L. M. "
Nevins, Edward "
Noel, J. S. "
Noblan, Jerry "
Nyswa, Morris.

Olmsted, Angeline.
Olinger, Oliver
O'Brient, Franklin
Paszewski, Wm.
Parsons, Alfred
Petch, Wm.
Pelton, J. O.
Parkhurst, J. G.
Phillips, H. S.
Patterson, V. M.
Prout, Lewis
Petch, Geo.
Peterson, James
Potter, Geo.
Potter, I. J.
Perkowski, Ruth E.
Pomson, F. M.
Ryder, Mrs. G. O.
Ryder, Francis
Roberts, John.
Rice, Samuel
Riggs, A. H.
Robinson, Warford.
Randall, S. B.
Roberts, D. M.
Rockwood, F. A.
Robinson, James.
Row, James.
Shipley, Levi
Randall, C. D.
Stevenson, H.
Shoecraft, B. B.
Shoecraft, Mrs. Mary
Shoecraft, Ezra.
Smith, M. A.
Spencer, Abram.
Sears, Edgar.
Searls, David.
Seeley, S. M.
Shoemaker, C. J.
Skelden, R. H.
Sanford, W. H.
Sanford, Alva.
Strickland, Jerome.
Sherwood, Solomon
Stevens, Alonzo
Straight, W. P.
Seely, Mrs. Anna.
Silver, George
Spring, Emerson
Slack, A. T.
Sperbeck, John.
Sabastion, L. C.
Snyder, Iron
Selleck, Larry.
Averill, John.
Sinclair, L.
Swaine, Albert.
Tucker, Mrs. Jane.
Treat, S. I.
Thompson, Thos.
Tucker, R. T.
Tramp, G. W.
Turner, G. H.
Tibbott, B. S.
Taylor, Oliver.
Trehane, U. G.
Taylor, Lewis.
Van Akms, J. H.
Ursborn, Percy.
Van Akms, Martha
Woodard, Otto
Wilson, W. H.
Whitney, J. W.
Wilson, Perry
Wood, J. O.
Waggart, Mrs. Roba.
Whitehead, Mrs G. H.
Wdren, Monroe
Williams, Mrs. John
Weimer, Mrs. W. H.
Willard, G. W.
Wyner, Wm.
Ward, John.
Welster, T. J.
Wood, Jason
Warren, H. O.
Wilder, Lewis.

Williams, G. H.
Weeks, Adelbert.
Webb, Ellen Jane.
Warford, Oak.
Young, Alexander
Zelewski, James.

Alger, Aromus R., Matteson
Alger, Orpha A., "
Allen, Cyrus M., "
Amba, Joseph, Sherwood.
Allen, I. O., Bronson
Allen, W. A., "
Allen, J. P., "
Asten, J. G., "
Blass, Chas., Orland, Ind.
Brainett, C. C., Bronson
Beach, H. P., Matteson
Benton, Herbert, "
Benton, Mrs. Olive, Bronson
Bare, Mrs. Mary, "
Bennett, Jas. M., Colon
Baker, John.
Baker, Lafayette, Matteson.
Bennett, John, "
Bennett, Mrs. Lizzie, "
Bathrick, Chas., Sherwood
Baxter, Chauncey A., Colon
Bathrick, M. K., Sherwood.
Ballou, Mrs. Bronson
Bean, Peter, Sherwood
Burnham, N. A., Bronson
Billings, Ames.
Bennett, Edwin R., Matteson
Bennett, Riley, Bronson.
Beers, Calvin, Colon.
Beers, H. H., "
Barkley, B. F., Matteson.
Benker, L. L., Bronson
Brownell, R. W., Colon.
Beech, Wm., Bronson.
Butterson, King, Sherwood
Bathrick, Seymour, "
Culver, O. B., Colon.
Coward, John, Matteson
Coward B. J., "
Carter, Cherry, Bronson
Conn, Geo., Colon.
Cunningham, Jas., Bronson
Colpetzer, Samuel, "
Colpetzer, Reuben, "
Carson Joseph, Matteson
Cushman, Mrs. C., "
Carter, John A., "
Corson, E. N., Bronson
Corson, Derrick, Bronson
Chapman, Amos, "
Corson, Mary O., "
Corson, S. B., "
Corson, J. W., Matteson
Corson, Jay C., "
Case, Willis, Bronson
Case, Lester, "
Copeland, R. K., Matteson
Crey, James, Bronson
Crey, Edgar, "
Coldren, Fred, Sherwood
Connor, Alva, Bronson.
Coddington, H. D., Sherwood.
Copeland, A. G., Colon.
Cradler, Frank, Bronson
Cook, Peter, Colon.
Culver, Chas., Matteson
Deens, Mrs. Kate, Bronson
Dunn, C. B., "
Danbury, G. R., Colon.
Dounsbury, John, Matteson
Dube, Marion, Bronson
Danvers, Dan'l, "
Dube, John, "
Dube, Mrs. Jane, "
Dupue, G. K., "
Decker, Sara, Colon.
Eberhard, Isaac, Colon
Rice, Joseph, Bronson
Eberhard, Chris., Colon
Eberhard, Homer, Bronson
Eberhard, Geo., Colon.
Eberhard, John, Burr Oak

Fish, E. C., Bronson
Fish, A. D., Colon
Fisk, M. M., "
Farewell, J. W., Sherwood.
Fordham, Lepis, Matteson.
Fish, Mrs. Ezra J., Bronson.
Foote, Brealy "
Frye, Henry, Colon.
French, John, Sherwood.
Farewell, Joseph, "
Fenno, Ross.
Goodwin, Seth F., Sherwood
Grover, Mrs. Mary, Matteson
Givin, Benjamin, Bronson.
Grey, Amos P., "
Gibbs, David, "
Guthrie, E. J., Colon.
Gravbadger, A., Bronson.
Gnogg, James, Colon.
Gibbs, Leonel, Bronson.
Gardner, Anson, Matteson.
Gardner, Sam'l, "
Greely, Chas., Bronson.
Gardner, Mrs. M., Colon.
Gabriel, John, Matteson.
Green, Mrs. R. F., Union City.
Guthrie, Hugh, Colon.
Hoyt, Thompson, Matteson.
Hoyt, Edward, "
Hogaboom, A. D., Colon.
Haws, Henry, Sherwood.
Hollister, A. S., Burr Oak.
Hunt, James H., Sherwood.
Hockett, Hiram Mrs., Bronson.
Hogaboom, C. T., Matteson.
Hogaboom, L. A., "
Hammond, Lydia, Colon.
Harger, Jeremiah, Mrs., Bronson.
Hassetter, W. F., Colon.
Hamlin, Erastus, Bronson.
Johnson, H. F., Matteson.
Johnson, R. A., "
Judd, A. C., "
Johnson, D. M., Bronson.
Jackson, J. D., Sherwood.
Jones, Leonander, Bronson.
Jones, George, Sherwood.
Jones, Isaac, Matteson.
Jackson, Andrew, Sherwood.
Kane, James, Colon.
Kane, Patrick, "
Kane, Thos., "
Lambenson, A., Colon
Lewis, Lorettos, Matteson
Lyter, George, Colon.
Lyter, Joseph, "
Lyter, Fred, "
Lyter, Reuben, "
Lyter Michael, "
Ladue, Mrs. Anna, Bronson.
Lytle, Jennie S., Sherwood.
Lytle, Bella A., "
Lyon, C. W., Colon.
Lilly, Henry M., Bronson.
Lock, James.
Lytle, John L., Colon.
Lare, Wellington, Bronson.
Lytle, G. B., Sherwood.
Lydle, Wilson, "
Mowry, Henry K., Sherwood
Monroe, Mrs. Sam, Burr Oak
McCarty, Wm. M., Colon.
McCarty, F. B., "
McLean, Hector, Bronson.
Myers, Michael, Colon.
Monroe, Geo., Bronson.
Mitchell, Byron, Union City.
Monroe, Jesse, Bronson.
McIntyre, Alex., Matteson
Miller, Wm. H., "
Mowry, Christopher, Athens
Mingus, Danforth, Sherwood.
Mingus, James, Colon.
Mills, Adolphus, Bronson.
Merlin, Henry Mrs., Colon
McLean, Judson, Bronson.
Mitchell, Eugene, Sherwood

BRONSON.

Harmon, Simon, Bronson
Harmon, Joseph, "
Harmon, Geo., "
Havens, Nathaniel "
Hollerck, S. "
Hopkins, E. J. "
Holmes, D., Mrs. "
Holmes, J. T. "
Hamilton, Chas. "
Hopelough, Dan'l "
Harris, H. "
Hoard, Chas. "
Hopelough, E., Noble
Holmes, C. J., Bronson
Hospingartner, John, Bronson
Havens, Arthur "
Harkins, H. "
Holbrook, E. H. "
Hall, Wm. "
Hoard Wm. "
Hinz, Isaac "
Hignuier, Earnest "
Junal, Josie, Bronson
Jones, Nicholas "
Jones, L. G. "
Jones, Frank "
James, Thos. "
Jump, Delos "
Jump, D. "
Johnson, Wm. "
Jepp, S. "
Jones, Ova "
Jones, Rettie "
Kalona, James, Bronson
Kabaash, Welenly "
Kalona, Andrew "
Kennedy, John "
Karn, Jacob "
Keys, C. L. "
Kean & Holmes "
Knapp, Wells "
Kolona, Michael "
Kons, Joseph "
Kennedy, Geo. "
Keaffar, R., Bronson
Kolone, Frank, Bronson
Kolone, Patrick "
Khine, David "
Kilahoski, John "
Keyes, Francis "
Krouka, J. "
Keyes, F. A. "
Klevinski, John "
Lott, L. M., Bronson
Leonard, A. B. "
Lane, V. "
Lewis, L. K., Mrs., Bronson
Lake, Aaron "
Latta, Joseph "
Latta, Mose "
Latta, Mary "
Lane, M. E., Mrs. "
Ladew, Martin "
Lombinski, Andrew "
Lewis, L. W. "
Loh, Martin "
Lyke, G. U. "
Lewis, Sarah "
Lewis, Judson "
Lambert, W., Batavia
Monroe, Wallace, Bronson
Monroe, Wm. "
Monroe, Jesse "
Mowry, H. P. "
Mogat, Chas. "
Moffill, A. M. "
Monroe, Darron "
Mallory, Helen "
Miller, A. A., Mrs. "
Monroe, Seth "
Millman, J. B. "
Millman, Mark "
Mallow, Geo. "
Malorn, John "
Millot, A. A. "
Modort, P. M. "
Monroe, Chas. "
Malorn, Andrew "
Modort, Peter "

Miller, Henry, Bronson
McQueen, M. "
Moore, M. J. "
Mowry, A. E. "
Malorn, Stephen "
Nichols, G. B. "
Nichols & Boughton "
Norton, Celista "
Needham, D. F., Coldwater
Olney, James, Bronson
Olney, H. J., Mrs., South Bend, Ind.
Outhouse, Fred., Coldwater
Parkham, A. K. "
Perham, Richard "
Park, J. B. "
Peeris, C. L. "
Post, Gridley "
Paul, Thomas "
Powers, Henry "
Powers, R. D. "
Pixley, A. "
Post, W. E., Mrs. "
Price, E. F. "
Pette, Peter "
Pullman, J. E. "
Fork, Mary E. "
Phillips, C. U. "
Pinney, Isaac "
Porter, Chas. "
Pierce, W. "
Price, Malinda "
Pixley, Isaac "

SUNFIELD OAK.

Parsons, Daniel
Queer, Lewis
Queer, Frank
Queer, Henry A.
Queer, Charles
Budd, F. M.
Ruple, A.
Ruple & Son
Roush, Jeavus
Richardson, A. J.
Ruggles, E. & A.
Reid S., Mrs.
Rose, L. A.
Robinson, L.
Ruggles, W. B.
Ruple, W. B.
Roseboom, G.
Robinson, Geo.
Rudd, Wm.
Sawson, S. W.
Ruggles, J. P.
Ruggles, Amelia
Richards, S. P.
Robinson, M.
Ruggles, Chas.
Ronell, J. H., Bronson
Rooney, John, Noble
Ruple & Shepard, Bronson
Roscell, Fria.
Sopright, S. S.
Ruple, W. H.
Saceria, Joseph
Rosenbrock, Geo.
Sirang, Chas.
Selby, R. Mrs.
Sielawski, M.
Sanders, La. H.
Sherwin, E., Mrs., Bronson
Shepard, A. M.
Sanborn, Henry
Shepard, Jason
Smith, Elizabeth
Smith, A. Y., Mrs.
Smith, Orva
Sherman, J., Bronson
Shepard, H. Y.
Smith, Wm.
Shaffmaster, C.
Simpson, Frank, Bronson
Shaffmaster, John
Sheffield, Geo., Bronson
Sheehly, M.
Shane, E., Mrs.
Sagar, Zad.
Smith, Chas.
Smith, John
Smith, Thos.

Secor, John, Bronson
Rhoonbacki, G. "
Stallwalk, V. "
Secor, James "
Shepp, Joseph "
Shippy, Eugene "
Swift, Albert "
Smoker, Frank "
Sweeting, Volney "
Shionski, Jacob "
Shaler, John "
Shaler, Geo. "
Sirackly, David "
Segar, Geo. "
Sagar, G. H. "
Sagar, Albert "
Sagar, Joseph "
Sagar, John "
Shaw, A. M., Mrs., Bronson
Shaw, Kreatus "
Simmae, Philip "
Shaw, J. H. "
Stedinger, John "
Selby, Wallace "
Sagar, Zed. "
Shedd, David "
Sheldon, Gustave "
Smoker, Joseph "
Shertz, John "
Sagar, John M. "
Shortz, Fred. "
Sagar, G. L. "
Thurlby, J. "
Thayer, Sam'l "
Teller, Miles "
Tice, Dan'l "
Troutdall, Wm. "
Tisdall, J. P., Mrs. "
Taggart, John "
Taggart, David "
Taggart, B. P. "
Thornton, A. F. "
Tice, Bert "
Ulrich, Cyrus, Bronson
Unterkircher, John "
Ulrich, John "
Vancotary, C. M., Sr. "
Vancotary, C. M., Jr. "
Van Fleet, A. S. "
Van Alsine, B. Mrs. "
Veazy, Henry "
Van Alsine, D. C. "
Vaweken, E. "
Van Vorst, C. C. "
Whitman, L. "
Warner, M. C. "
Williams, A. "
Whitaker, C. B. "
Whitaker & Corey "
Weldon, J. N. "
Whitaker, Dora "
Wood, Gyer "
Warner, J. A. "
Willy, J. C. "
Watson, A. B. "
Walker Bros. "
Wall, Henry "
Whitaker, Clara, Mt. Clemens, Mich.
Wrobloski, M., Bronson
Wrobloski, Jacob "
Warner, Adam "
Walker, Wm. "
Weaver, J. W. "
Walters, S. "
Weck, Frank "
Whitaker, A., Mrs. "
Walker, Orange "
Werner, J. P. "
Walden, Elmer "
Towash, Anton "
Zimmerman, Lenora, "

QUINCY.

Aldrich, A. E.
Allen, J. P.
Anthony, W. L.
Andrews, N. H.
Alexander, J. D.
Arnold, Green
Ashton, Isaac
Ashton, Corbett
App, D. W.
Babcock, John
Babcock, G. D.
Babcock, Lucy
Barlor, Marshall
Barbor, A. W.
Barbor, D. H.
Baker, H. C.
Baker, V. E.
Ball, P. C.
Ball, Lucy E.
Barker, J. H.
Barnes, Joel
Barnes, Thos. N.
Barnes, W. J.
Benjamin, Isaac
Becker, Jeremiah
Benbow, Wm.
Belote, A. J.
Barnes, C A H.
Bennett, J. C.
Bennett, Hiram
Bennett, H. H.
Bennett, C. W.
Bennett, G. E.
Bender, Jacob
Bowles, Geo.
Berry, J. H.
Bierly, Mrs. Ezra
Burson, John
Bunnell, G. H.
Bulltock, Alex
Born, G. O.
Bowerman, Granville
Bowerman, Isaac
Bowerman, Elisha
Bowen, A. L.
Bowen, E. T.
Bowen, E. W.
Banger, Herbert
Bowen, Mrs. M.
Byerton, S. U.
Bingham, W. N.
Blackmer, P.
Brown, M. M.
Brown, L. B.
Brinkley, Franz & Geo.
Brinkley, May
Brinkley, J. C.
Briggs, L.
Corbus, Leonard
Corbus, Fred.
Corbus, Jacob
Corbus, Jason
Corbus, Geo.
Corwin, Wm.
Craner, Melissa
Craine, Morris
Crawford, Wm.
Crapo, Elizabeth
Croorb, M.
Croorb, Chas.
Culver, F. J.
Culver, J. J.
Culver, Mrs. W. H. H.
Culver, Helen
Culver, Abram
Chase, C. H.
Cummings, Jesse
Curtin, Wm.
Carroll, C. B.
Caldwell, Seymore
Cuoy, Nancy
Cooie, Benj.
Dalley, Romain
Day, Geo.
Day, D. C.
Darling, Ella
Durker, Geo.
Durker, Mary
Decker, N. N.
Denham, Horton
Dean, Mrs. N. E.
Delcmeter, H. S.
Denham, N. H.
Denham, Ruth
Denham, M. L.
Dickonson, A. B.
Dickonson, M. M.
Dickonson, Mrs. C.

www.ingramcontent.com/pod-product-compliance
Lightning Source LLC
Chambersburg PA
CBHW022340020726
47500CB00004B/1202